THE RING
THE SPANIARD
GAVE HER

LYNNE GRAHAM

MILLS & BOON

First published in Great Britain 2021
by Mills & Boon, an imprint of HarperCollins*Publishers* Ltd,
1 London Bridge Street, London, SE1 9GF

www.harpercollins.co.uk

HarperCollins*Publishers*
1st Floor, Watermarque Building,
Ringsend Road, Dublin 4, Ireland

Large Print edition 2021

The Ring the Spaniard Gave Her © 2021 Lynne Graham

ISBN: 978-0-263-28879-7

08/21

MIX
Paper from
responsible sources
FSC™ C007454

This book is produced from independently certified FSC™ paper to ensure responsible forest management. For more information visit www.harpercollins.co.uk/green.

Printed and bound in Great Britain
by CPI Group (UK) Ltd, Croydon, CR0 4YY

THE RING
THE SPANIARD
GAVE HER

CHAPTER ONE

RUY VALIENTE, THE reclusive billionaire owner of Valiente Capital, one of the world's largest and most successful hedge funds, didn't immediately answer his mobile when it pulsed in his pocket.

Why? He was in a great mood, happily contemplating a few weeks off finance and the opportunity to indulge in his secret passion. Those breaks were both rare and precious in his life because he had been brought up to be enormously disciplined and do his duty. He was also in transit to his rural English home, which he planned to make his very private bolt-hole. When he finally grudgingly drew out the phone, bearing in mind that a call to his personal number—known to few—could be an emergency, he was reassured when he saw his half-sister, Cecile's name flash up.

In his rigorously conservative, judgemental circle of relations, Cecile was just about the only one he could stomach, and it was to her that he owed the discovery of his new home, he reminded himself as he answered.

'I need your help,' Cecile told him without any preamble. 'And I know it's a dreadful imposition and that when you're moving into a house only a couple of miles away from Charles and me you will now suspect that we're going to be a nuisance—'

Ruy smiled. 'That thought would never occur to me.'

'Where are you?' she asked.

'Ten minutes from my new house.'

'Oh, good. Charles and I are stuck in a jam on the motorway. We were on our way home early to see the girls perform in their spring concert,' she told him. 'But we're not going to make it in time.'

'That's unfortunate.' Ruy was sympathetic because his sister and her husband were medics, whom he knew often struggled to combine work and family commitments. 'How can I help?'

'Lola and Lucia will be devastated when we don't turn up. They've been rehearsing their performance for weeks,' Cecile told him tautly. 'I know it's a very big ask, Ruy, because it's not your sort of thing, but if you could show up in our stead it would mean a lot to the girls. In fact, your appearance would be much more exciting than ours. Tio Ruy is hugely popular with them. The concert is in the village hall and it's already started. Luckily, the girls are in the very last act. Can you make it?'

Ruy swallowed every one of the objections brimming on his lips and murmured, 'Of course I can,' because it was the very *first* time his half-sister had asked him for anything.

All the rest of his relatives maintained a constant barrage of requests for money, jobs, help with legal and family problems—indeed every bump in the road of their lives from disease to divorce inspired their urgent pleas for assistance. Of course, his late father, Armando, had encouraged that dependency on the head of the Valiente family because it had fed his love of power and a subservient audience, but Ruy found that same steady stream of demands exasperating and was gradually doing what he could to discourage his relations from the habit.

'You...*will*?' Cecile could hide neither the relief nor the surprise in her response. 'You won't need to take the girls home or anything. Their nanny is with them. All you have to do is show your face and give them a hug afterwards and obviously *lie* when Lola asks how she did because she's like a baby elephant on stage...bless her! It shouldn't take more than an hour of your time.'

'It's fine, Cecile.'

'But this is your first visit to your new home and I'm totally invading your privacy,' she protested guiltily.

'I'm not that inflexible,' he assured her soothingly, although he knew that he was lying out of courtesy. He had learned the hard way over his thirty years that if he didn't ruthlessly carve out the time for his art from his incredibly demanding schedule in the world of investment, he didn't get *any* time to do what he most enjoyed. 'It will be good to see the girls.'

'If you would only agree to visit us more often…sorry, in a moany mood here,' Cecile mumbled apologetically, knowing that she was crossing his boundaries.

Ruy was very much a loner who cherished his privacy, a privilege he saw little of in the real world where he was invariably surrounded by staff. Employees waited on him hand and foot and hung on his every word and, all credit to him, he *was* aware that his lifestyle was far from normal. He was also rather more painfully aware that his twin brother, Rodrigo, his junior only by a matter of minutes, was consumed by envy, resentment and bitterness that he had not been the firstborn son, on whom all Armando Valiente's brightest hopes and expectations rested. It was a terrible ironic truth that Ruy would have very much preferred the far less demanding role of younger son and brother. And it struck him as even worse that his brother had asked him to his wedding to take place in a fortnight and that he was dreading the event, unable to unquestioningly accept that the invitation could be an olive branch.

The community hall beside the church was an old shabby building in need of a facelift, Ruy registered. He would consider making an anonymous donation. Philanthropic gestures came naturally to a man who had never in his life had to consider the cost of anything. It would also be the first time that Ruy actually set foot in the village near the property he had bought. There wasn't much to the place: a garage, a little supermarket and, opposite the church, a pub with a big flashy sign that said it had pretensions to be something more. On his one previous visit, he had driven through the village without stopping because it didn't interest him. He had no plans to get to know anyone in the neighbourhood, a decision that would protect the anonymity he treasured.

There were no empty seats available in the packed hall, which suited Ruy fine. He stationed himself by the back wall, his height of six feet four granting him an excellent view of the small stage, which was currently in darkness. Strange plinky-plonky music notes filtered out, the kind of New Age stuff that made Ruy, who liked rock ballads, wince. A low light came on above the silhouette of a woman kneeling with her head bent. Unexpected interest fired in him as the music swelled and the woman began to unfold. Like a flower in one of those sped up nature documentaries, he thought abstractedly.

As her arms lifted in a fluid shimmy, she leant back, seemingly as flexible as rubber, her long hair fluttering, her small full breasts jutting up, her body bending back in a natural curve. Ruy was riveted to the spot, only dimly aware of the children, crouched like little mushrooms awaiting their moment in the darkness, to either side of her. It was modern dance, again something he had no interest in, but the innocent sensuality of her every move captured him as both a man and an artist. She slowly rose upright, hands moving like silent poetry, her grace phenomenal and that fast he knew he had to find out who she was, knew he *had* to paint her.

'She's a firecracker,' a male voice commented next to him. 'A beauty.'

'Who is she?' Ruy didn't know whether or not she was a beauty because her entire performance had taken place in shadow; as if she were part of the backdrop and not the centre of the show, which would definitely be wishful thinking on her part if that had been the intention, he reflected with wry amusement, considering that she was the most eye-catching sight he had enjoyed in a very long time.

'Suzy Madderton, publican's daughter, well and truly off the market if you're interested.'

'I wasn't,' Ruy asserted, unusual colour slashing his high cheekbones because he was shamed by the throb at his groin in a place where children were present, even though in the darkness nobody could have seen or noticed his condition.

'Heard she's getting hitched soon and to a golden oldie, *not* a young chap like yourself… know what I mean,' the older man imparted. 'Local businessman, owns half the village… a crying shame *her* ending up with *him*!'

Ruy said nothing, too cynical after the life he had led to think it even remotely strange that a young and apparently beautiful woman would marry an older man for his money. His only concern was whether or not he could get her to model for him, and if money were a magnet that would be his 'in'.

He wouldn't touch a gold-digger with a bargepole, not that he had any personal interest in the dancer. A natural male response to a sensual performance was no proof of attraction, he assured himself. After all, sex was no big deal to Ruy and hadn't been in a long time. Casual sex was easily available to him and he hadn't been on a date in longer than he could recall. Love was anathema to him because he had witnessed and experienced how warped and damaged love could become. Someone like his former sister-in-law, Liliana, could get badly burned by that seemingly desirable emotion of love that so many foolish beings chased. Old unforgotten guilt burned in Ruy's gut as he watched his nieces dance across the stage as very cute little mushrooms. Lucia was sylph-like in comparison to poor little Lola, who stomped like a water buffalo. Slowly, almost painfully, Ruy smiled, reflecting that if it didn't entail getting married, he would have enjoyed having a child of his own…

'Reckon you raised a dad temperature or two out there!' Flora, the concert organiser, teased Suzy as she hurriedly pulled on her clothes at the back of the stage. 'The men can't take their eyes off you.'

'Nonsense, they're just keen to spot their kids,' Suzy declared, a little nauseous at the prospect of being the target of lust in public. Wasn't it bad enough that she had had to recently cope with it in private?

She squashed that self-pitying thought as soon as it popped up in the back of her brain.

Hadn't she chosen her own path? Hadn't she decided to put her dad first? Her dad, the man who had loved her enough for two parents after her mother died in a car crash when she was a toddler. Roger Madderton was a great father, just not quite farsighted enough to see when a trap was being sprung in front of him. And Percy Brenton had caught both father and daughter in a hellish financial trap and there was no escaping the consequences of that miscalculation. Either she let her father go bankrupt through no fault of his own, and watched him lose his home and business, or she married Percy. And as she was marrying Percy in less than forty-eight hours, she had best settle down and accept the inevitable, she told herself irritably. By the weekend, she would be in Barbados on her honeymoon with Percy, and she cringed at the prospect.

The concert was over. People were already starting to leave as Suzy descended the stage steps. In her haste her rich auburn hair bounced against her spine in a flyaway mop of curls. Lola and Lucia came running across the floor to greet her, full of excitement after their performance. They were the cutest little girls, one seven, one four, and they were in the dance class that Suzy taught every week. Even though she was keen to escape the hall before Percy could put in an appearance, she couldn't resist the little hands grabbing hold of hers and pulling her forward. Laughing, green eyes sparkling with mirth at their enthusiasm, Suzy found herself looking, not at the parents she expected or even the nanny, but at a tall, dark total stranger.

A tall, dark, quite magnificent stranger, she adjusted, her tongue sticking to the roof of her mouth, because he was breathtakingly handsome. Olive-tinted skin stretched taut over a superb bone structure that formed the perfect backdrop to spare, flaring cheekbones, a sculpted jawline shadowed with a blue-black hint of stubble, a classic nose and wide, sensual lips. Add in his height and lean, powerful build and he came as close to a fantasy male as Suzy had ever seen in reality.

Beautiful wasn't an expressive enough

word to describe Suzy Madderton, Ruy conceded, taken aback by her sheer visual impact. She glowed like a spectacular sunset with her vibrant copper-red spirals of hair, porcelain-pale skin, a scattering of freckles across the bridge of her small nose and green eyes brighter than polished emeralds. Spirit and energy bubbled out of her. All his defensive antennae came into play, snapping up his reserve like a safety barrier because Ruy instantly loathed the strength of his response to her. Even worse, he was deeply uneasy around any woman he sensed to be volatile in the emotional field.

'Tio Ruy!' Lola proclaimed importantly. '*Our* Tio Ruy!'

'Their mother's brother, their uncle,' Ruy interpreted smoothly.

Suzy was ensnared by eyes as dark as Hades and full of sardonic superiority. She didn't know why or how she read that message in his stunningly dark gaze, but she did, and her chin came up at an angle, her eyes sparkling with animosity. 'Thanks for the translation but I didn't need it. My mother was Spanish. I have a few words,' she murmured, thinking it was *very* few words, even after the evening classes she had attended for years, because lack of practice had killed her hope of becoming fluent in her mother's language.

Everything that was masculine and proud in Ruy thrilled to that unexpected challenge and he had all the pride of his *hidalgo* forebears. A firecracker, yes, he could *see* that in the aggressive lift of her delicate chin, the toss of her shamelessly untidy hair. She wouldn't suit his needs at all in the sex department, he acknowledged without hesitation. He preferred his women neat, meek and mild and unlikely to cause waves, but that didn't mean that he didn't *still* want her as a model. After all, he had barely spoken to his last model, now world-famous thanks to the exposure of his previous year's exhibition because his portraits of beautiful women sold for millions. He didn't do involvement in any part of his life and that was how he avoided the messy chaos of emotions that had once engulfed him in family disaster.

He spoke to Suzy in Spanish too fast for her to follow in detail and she only got the gist of what he was saying. He was offering her a job as a model. An artist's model. *Her?* Suzy couldn't believe her ears and marvelled that the girls' friendly outgoing mother, Cecile, hadn't mentioned the fact that her brother was an artist or that he had come to stay with her.

'Name your price,' he said to conclude in English, wanting to be sure she got that message. 'It would only take a couple of weeks of your time.'

A heavy arm fell round Suzy's shoulders and her heart sank instantly to the soles of her biker boots: Percy had arrived. 'Price for what?' he demanded.

'I was asking Miss Madderton if she would consider acting as an artist's model for me.' Ruy extended his hand politely to Percy. 'Ruy Rivera,' he murmured, borrowing his illegitimate half-sister's maiden name to assure his anonymity. When he was in artist mode and he wanted to be anonymous, he generally used Rivera as a name to cover his tracks.

'That is absolutely out of the question, Mr Rivera,' Percy announced with crushing contempt as he ignored Ruy's extended hand. 'Suzy and I are getting married the day after tomorrow. She'll be far too busy!'

'You could have been nicer to him. He didn't mean any offence,' Suzy whispered in sheer embarrassment as Percy herded her domineeringly towards the exit, affecting not to hear the sallies aimed at her from other people.

Angry fingers bit into her upper arm. 'Don't tell *me* how to behave!' her fiancé snapped in her ear as he thrust her bodily in the direction of his car. 'And that'll be the end of all this dance nonsense now. I'm not having my wife up on a stage showing herself off to all and sundry like some stripper!' he practically spat at her.

Pale and shivering in the cold air, shaken by his anger, Suzy stepped away from him in the direction of the street while rubbing

at her arm. 'You hurt me,' she muttered unevenly. 'I haven't done anything. Why are
you so annoyed?'

'Stop making a fuss, Suzy. Get in the car,'
Percy told her impatiently. 'You'll come home
with me and get some supper.'

'I'm sorry. I'm really tired after all that…
er…dancing,' Suzy lied, screening a fake
yawn with a slender hand, her wary gaze
pinned to the older man's flushed and still furious face. Supper was merely a euphemism
for groping in Percy's parlance and he had
agreed months ago to her demand that theirs
would be a marriage in name only. Whether
or not he had believed he could change her
mind on that score, she had no idea, but she
had no plans to engage in an additional war
of words and resentment on his sofa after the
roughness with which he had handled her.
'As you said, I have a lot to do for the wedding, so I'll just head home now. Thanks,' she
completed stiffly, wondering what she was
thanking him for but dismayed by the rage

in his bloodshot blue eyes and knowing that she was trying to placate him.

'Suzy!' Her father's wonderfully familiar voice hailed her, and she turned in relief to greet him.

Percy took a step back, a forced smile settling on his florid face. 'Roger,' he said quietly, all hint of the rage wiped from his expression.

'Where did you come from?'

'I ran over to see your dance and stood at the exit watching,' her father confided. 'I wouldn't miss you for the world.'

'But who's been watching the bar?' she asked.

'Old Man Morgan was left in charge,' he said with a smile as he named an elderly local who was practically a fixture in the bar and guided her across the road to the pub. 'Everything all right between you and Percy?'

Suzy stiffened. 'Yes...why are you asking?'

'From a distance it looked like you were having a quarrel,' the older man admitted, looking anxious. 'I reckon I'm being ridiculous but, for an instant there, I honestly thought he was about to *hit* you!'

Suzy was pale as milk as she stepped into the familiar heat of the pub where a log fire burned in the stone fireplace and where only one customer propped up the bar. 'Yes, that is ridiculous,' she told him firmly. 'Percy wouldn't do anything like that.'

'He looked like he'd been drinking as well and he must be drinking at home or at his hotel because he doesn't do any drinking here,' he pointed out worriedly. 'Are you sure about this marriage?'

'Yes… I can't wait to see Barbados!' she teased, hoping to take him off the subject.

Roger Madderton groaned and brushed a straying strand of red hair off her pale brow. 'It doesn't feel right to me…me owing him money, you marrying him, him saying I don't need to repay it now, like it's nothing, when he's known to be as tight as a drum with his cash!'

'Well, Percy's right that you shouldn't have money owing between family members, and after the wedding it *will* feel more normal,' she assured her father confidently.

'I still feel that he's too old for you,' Roger admitted. 'He's almost as old as I am, for goodness' sake, no spring chicken, and you wouldn't catch me chasing a woman half my age!'

'Everyone's different and Percy will give me a good life.'

Roger grimaced. 'If I taught you that a good life had to encompass a big house and foreign holidays, I failed somewhere along the line.'

'Dad...' Reluctant to tell him any more cover-up lies, Suzy hugged the older man. 'Stop being silly. You are the very best father any woman could ever want.'

'I'm sorry. All I want is to see you happy and I'm not convinced Percy can give you that.'

'You'll be convinced eventually!' Suzy quipped as she headed for the rear door that led into the apartment where they lived, not entirely convinced that Old Man Morgan was as deaf as he seemed. At the end of the day all that she cared about was her father's happiness and security and marrying Percy would ensure that.

Suzy went upstairs to bed, thinking about all the sacrifices her father had made to raise her alone. There hadn't ever been any other woman in his life because he had been afraid that he might give her one of those wicked stepmothers straight out of fiction. He had always worked very long hours striving to make the bar a success and it genuinely wasn't his fault that he was deep in debt.

His problems had begun years ago, after he had borrowed from the bank to renovate the pub in the forlorn hope that it would encourage more customers. When the loan payments had become too much, and he had fallen behind, the bank had threatened to foreclose on him. That was when Percy had come in, softly, softly like a thief in the night, she reflected with a faint shudder of recollection. Back then she had only been eighteen, incapable of seeing that Percy had undoubtedly always intended to take her father's business from him and that it was possible that she had only been an afterthought. Percy had been Roger's hero then, taking on the debt and offering lower repayments.

And then one day six months ago, just before her twenty-first birthday, Percy had stopped to give her a lift in the village and he had laid out the facts for her without an ounce of shame. He had threatened to repossess the pub and evict them unless Suzy agreed to marry him. When she had accused him of blackmail, he had made much of the fact that he was offering her the respectability of matrimony and an infinitely more comfortable life than she currently enjoyed, working all hours in the pub as she did, cleaning, cooking and tending the bar. To balance the scales, Suzy had agreed to marry him but she had also insisted that, while she would act as a wife in every other field, she wanted her own bedroom and their union would not include sex. At the time, Percy had agreed, but more recently she had begun to suspect that he regretted that pact and resented her for her refusal to share a bed with him.

Suzy curled up in a tight ball in her bed, burning tears of regret forcing a passage from beneath her eyelids. Had she realised six months ago just how difficult it would be to marry a man she didn't love and whom she wasn't remotely attracted to? No, back then, she'd had no real idea of what she was signing up for and now it was too late. She felt trapped but she had *agreed* to be trapped. Either she told her father the truth and they ended up homeless and broke or she married Percy. Percy, who was suddenly getting rough with her, which frightened her more than she wanted to admit.

Having parted from his nieces, Ruy climbed back into his vehicle, a purely practical choice that would not attract the particular notice that a fancier car or limousine and driver would. He was still marvelling that a young woman as striking as Suzy Madderton could choose to marry an ignorant loudmouth of a bully such as the man he had met. But it was none of his business and had he not still desired to paint her he was convinced he would have thought no more of her. As it was, however, he was unaccustomed to meeting with the word no and running into an obstacle only made him all the more obstinately determined to get what he wanted. Once he was settled into his new property, he would call into the pub and speak to Suzy alone, he decided with satisfaction. Women who said no to Ruy were so rare as to be non-existent.

For the two days before the wedding, Suzy was run off her feet. There was a final fitting for her gown. She was not having any attendants, no bridal party as such, having decided that the fewer people dragged into her masquerade of being a happy bride, the easier it would be. In any case, all her school friends had long since disappeared to go to college or look for jobs unavailable in a rural village, options that had never really been a possibility for Suzy. Besides the dress fitting, which entailed a long drive into the nearest town and took up the entire morning, she had to call into Percy's country house hotel, which lay several miles outside the village and where the reception was being held, to check arrangements, and she also had to pick up the cake and deliver it. She was doing the flowers in the church with the florist that evening. All else completed, she returned to the pub and was taken aback to see Ruy Rivera lounging by the fire there with a whisky and a broadsheet newspaper.

The first time she had seen him he had been wearing a beautifully tailored suit and she had wondered vaguely if he had been at a wedding or some similar event, but on this occasion he was casually clad in jeans and a knit sweater the colour of oatmeal. His hair, blue black as a raven's wing and equally glossy and thick, was ruffled back from his bronzed brow, a little longer in length than was strictly conservative. In that first glance she registered afresh that he was so gorgeous he literally stole the breath from her lungs and made her mouth run dry. Fierce embarrassment claimed her as she glanced down at the sparkling solitaire on her engagement finger. Whatever else she owed Percy, she firmly believed that she owed him her loyalty and respect, and looking with interest at another man, no matter how hot he was, felt entirely wrong.

Her fair skin deeply flushed by guilty pink, she stepped behind the bar to give her father a break.

'I thought you were at the church doing the flowers,' Roger Madderton said in surprise.

'The florist changed the time. She has another booking to cover first,' Suzy explained. 'Go and get your tea.'

'Yes, your bossiness.' Her father chuckled and sped off through the door into their living quarters.

Ruy folded his newspaper and vaulted upright to approach the bar. 'I was hoping that you would appear.'

Crystalline green eyes glimmered over him as though reluctant to land or linger. 'What can I get you? Another whisky?'

'No, thank you. I'm driving,' Ruy murmured with perfect diction, his Spanish accent purring along the syllables like an expensive sports car, she heard herself think foolishly of his dark, deep, oh-so-masculine drawl. 'Would it be rude for me to ask about your Spanish mother?'

Disconcerted, Suzy stilled, her eyes reflective. 'No, not at all. I don't remember her because she died in a car crash when I was two. She was from Madrid and she lost her parents when she was quite young. She came to the UK as an au pair and met my father. They were married within months. I took Spanish classes because I wanted to feel closer to her, but it doesn't really work if you don't get to practise speaking the language.' She sighed.

'You could practise on me,' Ruy suggested. 'How long have you been giving dance lessons to the local kids?'

'A couple of years now, first as an assistant until the teacher, who taught me for years, retired because of her arthritis. Dancing was my only hobby growing up,' Suzy admitted.

'I'm still hoping that you'll act as a model for me. I really *would* like to paint you.'

'I'm sorry but it's not possible. I'm getting married tomorrow and then I'll be away on my honeymoon for a couple of weeks and, in any case, Percy wouldn't agree to it.'

'You don't strike me as a young woman who always does as she's told. I'm willing to wait a few weeks to paint you,' Ruy volunteered.

'I can't do it and that's that. Will you please drop the subject now?' Suzy shot back at him in exasperation. 'Don't you know how to take no for an answer?'

A slashing smile slanted Ruy's wide mobile lips. 'No,' he dared.

Suzy's teeth gritted. 'Well, it's a very annoying trait…yes, sir…what can I get you?' she asked another man who had wandered up to the bar and went to serve him.

Ruy was unused to being left to kick his heels; it was his turn to grit teeth. Just at that moment faking being a more ordinary mortal wasn't working well for him. The usual awe, flattery and flirtation that women gave him would have been remarkably welcome just then. *Hombre!* A barmaid was giving him lip! His half-sister's voice sounded in his conscience and he knew she would have told him that he was being both snobbish and unjust. Cecile, ignored and hidden by their father as the daughter of his mistress, had had a much rougher ride through life than Ruy had ever had, and he had a sneaking suspicion that his opinionated and down-to-earth sibling would have laughed at seeing him being ignored and cold-shouldered by a woman.

'One last word on the subject?' Ruy breathed softly as she moved closer to him while wiping the bar top.

'Name your price for being my model and I will pay it,' he murmured in sibilant conclusion.

'You're just inviting me to pluck some sum of money out of the air? I haven't a clue what artists' models charge!' Suzy objected.

'I want you, nobody else, which gives you a

truly rare and special value,' Ruy told her. 'I will pay a *huge* sum for you to model for me.'

Suzy dealt him a frowning glance of reluctant fascination. 'That's crazy. There *has* to be a limit.'

'Not with me, there's not,' Ruy assured her stubbornly, forgetting in that instant that he was not in his own world of gilded exclusivity where nothing cost too much and nothing he desired was ever out of his reach.

Suzy wondered what it was about her that made men try to buy her. Percy had already done it, she reminded herself wretchedly. She could only think of the horrific sum her father had been told he owed after Percy had added on the interest charges that her poor father had misunderstood how to calculate. 'Fifty thousand pounds,' she said mockingly. 'I'll do it for—'

'That's a deal, then,' Ruy declared with intense satisfaction, relieved that money was the lure he had assumed it would be because it made him more conscious of the barrier between them, a barrier he was determined to maintain.

Suzy's brows rose at that response and she surveyed him in complete stupefaction. 'You expect me to *believe* that you can pay me fifty thousand pounds to act as your model? Like you're some Mr Rockefeller or something? Do I look like I still believe in Santa Claus and the tooth fairy?' She gulped with a sudden helpless giggle of appreciation. 'Oh, thank you, *thank you* for winding me up like that! I needed something to laugh about tonight and that offer was, not only tasteless, but also absolutely priceless!'

Ruy stared back at her in angry astonishment, never before having met anyone who failed to take him very seriously indeed. It was an instant when he surprised himself, learning that he was, in spite of all the many times he had assured himself he was not, a Valiente down to the backbone, proud of his blue-blooded heritage, his power and influence and arrogant as all get-out. He wouldn't let himself notice how laughter transformed her face from pure Madonna perfection to girlish natural amusement, eyes lighting up like stars, pale slender throat extending, that full pink cupid's bow mouth that tantalised him pouting in a delicious pillowy curve.

Percy stalked through the door, his mouth tightening when he saw his fiancée laughing behind the bar with Ruy leaning on it.

Unable to judge his mood as he stood in the shadows by the door, Suzy smiled at her fiancé and said, 'I thought I wasn't to see you tonight. I'm going over to do the flowers as soon as Dad comes back.'

'I'll see you there,' Percy declared curtly and swung on his heel to leave again.

Suzy breathed in deep and slow to soothe herself, recognising that she was in an anxious, volatile mood because she couldn't stop thinking about her wedding the next day and her nerves and regrets were really beginning to eat her alive. Making a sacrifice, even for someone that you loved as she loved her father, was much harder than she had thought it would be months earlier…

CHAPTER TWO

THE FLORIST, NOT PERCY, was waiting for Suzy when she crossed the road to walk into the picturesque little church. It was unusually cold for a spring evening and she shivered, wishing she had thought to put on a coat. The florist was in a hurry and had already positioned her arrangements by the time that Suzy arrived, leaving the bride to do nothing more than make her own few personal touches.

'It looks wonderful,' she told the older woman as she left, contriving a generous smile because it wasn't the woman's fault that Suzy was a less than happy bride-to-be. She hurried about tying small floral beribboned tokens to the ends of the pews. Her bridegroom had paid for everything and had spared no expense, although Suzy had not made a single extravagant choice for an event that she had feared taking place. Way back at the beginning, after his blackmailing start, though, Percy had been polite and reasonably pleasant but in recent months, as they got closer to the wedding, he had become terse and more difficult to deal with.

Sadly, however, her father's debt would not be written off until she became Percy's legally wedded wife. Could she honestly trust the older man to continue to respect the terms they had agreed, though? Right now, she was getting a little nervous about being alone with Percy behind closed doors, forced to tolerate his moods and hope for the best. Perhaps if she had been more sexually experienced she might have been less nervous of the older man, she reasoned uncertainly. Then she might have been more confident that she could accurately read his behaviour. But Suzy was a virgin, less from choice than from lack of opportunity, living in a small place where she met few single men.

Hearing a noise in the church porch, she

grabbed her bag and went to switch off the lights, assuming it was Percy and wondering what on earth he wanted to see her about so late in the day. As she walked out into the dim porch, she was grabbed by both shoulders and flung back against the hard stone wall like a doll and a stifled shriek of fear erupted from her. She thought she was being attacked and then she saw Percy squaring up to her with a pugnacious face of fury.

'What the heck?' she began in disbelief.

Percy clamped a silencing hand to her mouth. 'Standing there at the bar flirting with another man…making a fool of me, were you?' he growled at her.

'No, we weren't flirting… I swear,' she declared shakily, sincerely afraid of the way he was behaving and eager to placate him so that he would free her. 'The silly man was still trying to persuade me to model for him—'

'You're lying, just like Barb did!' he thundered down at her, unimpressed.

'Who's Barb?' Suzy whispered, her spine

and her head still stinging from that first rough meeting with the wall.

'My first wife and I'm not having another one like her, running after all the men, making a mockery of me round the neighbourhood!' he spat down at her, his eyes locked on her with what looked very like hatred to her frightened gaze.

'Please let me go, Percy,' Suzy whispered because, while Percy might not be a very tall man, he was built like an ox, square and stocky and strong. 'This has got out of hand.'

'Shut up…you don't tell me what to do… *ever*!' he launched down at her, slapping her across the face in a glancing blow that caused her head to strike the wall behind her again and extracted a gasp of pain from her pale lips. 'Not so cheeky now, are you? I've been too soft with you.'

'Let me go,' Suzy urged between clenched teeth. 'This is assault, Percy, and I won't stand for it!'

And he laughed as though she had said the funniest thing he had ever heard.

'What are you planning to do about it? Report me to the police when I can throw you and your dad out of this village any time I like? I own you just as I own all the businesses round here and don't you forget it!' Percy lifted his hands off her with an exaggerated flourish. 'I've gone easy on you this time. Don't let me see you flirting like that again!'

Suzy was so dizzy, she staggered as she slid back down the wall onto her own feet again. He was a frighteningly strong man because he had held her suspended all that time, but then she was a small and slender woman. As Percy slammed noisily into the car he had left parked across the street, she lifted her bag from where it had fallen and headed back home, praying her father would already be in bed. She massaged her aching head as she crept upstairs to her room. All of her ached from being thrown against the wall and her face was still stinging from that blow.

In the mirror she saw that she had had a nosebleed. She was in shock, trembling and staring at her drained and distraught face. She cleaned herself up in the bathroom, noting that her face was swollen while wondering how much make-up it would take to hide what might well be a bruise by morning. In her bra and pants she inspected her body and recognised the purple bruising already becoming visible on her arms and shoulders. She hugged herself and shuddered.

Percy had been married before and nobody local was aware of that fact. He was violent and territorial and had seen flirtation where none existed. But she still had to marry him, *didn't she*? She had to have that debt cleared for her dad and, once that was achieved, if Percy laid his hands on her again she would go to the police. On that decision she went to bed.

In the morning she went by rote through her bridal preparations. Her gown was all lace, ribbons and glittering crystals because Percy had instructed her to buy 'something fancy' and the ultra-feminine frills were the sort of thing that Percy deemed fancy. Fortunately, the long sleeves hid her bruises and cosmetics took care of her bruised cheekbone. But as she finally looked at herself in the mirror it was as if she were only then emerging from a waking nightmare: suddenly she knew she *couldn't* go through with the wedding—not for her dad, not for any reason could she face marrying a man who clearly believed that it was his right to beat her up.

'Hey, love, I'm just off down to the off-licence for later… OK? I'll only be half an hour,' her father told her from outside the door. 'We've got plenty of time.'

She yanked open the door and gave him a hug. 'I love you,' she told him, but she didn't have the courage to tell him that she was about to leave Percy at the altar. She would write a note but there could be no explanation because her father would kill Percy if he knew what he had done to his daughter and she didn't want to cause a fight in which her much smaller father might get hurt.

She was going to run. She had no car, not even a bike and very little money, her brain reminded her. Where was she planning to go? What she was hoping to do? But just at that moment the practicalities honestly didn't matter to her. All that mattered to her was that she had finally made a decision and that there would be less dangerous fallout all round if she simply vanished. In haste she wrote a note to her father, telling him that she was sorry, but she simply couldn't go through with the wedding and that she'd phone him as soon as she was able. No note necessary for Percy. When she failed to show he would know that he had shown his true colours too clearly to her the night before. She kicked off her bridal heels and reached for her biker boots.

As she was bending over, tightening the multicoloured laces, her attention fell on the window and the view across to the church. She saw Percy climbing out of his car in a dark suit and then turning to stare across at the pub. *Why* was he arriving so early for the ceremony? Did he already suspect that she might not turn up?

Sheer dread grabbed Suzy as she won-

dered if he would try to see her, *check* on her.
Her stomach heaved with nausea, her brow
banged with stress. The bag she had been
planning to pack, the clothing she had been
meaning to change into…it all totally fled
her mind and panic took over instead, washing away every other consideration, including
common sense. Grabbing her bag, she pulled
out her purse and extracted what cash she
had within it. Thrusting the banknotes she
had down the front of her dress into her bra,
she simply ran down the stairs and out into
the beer garden, which was surrounded by
the dense woods that ringed the village. She
had run wild in those woods as a child and,
even in the cold air with actual snowflakes
starting to fall, they had never looked more
enticing to her than they did at that moment.

Hoisting her full skirts high round her legs,
Suzy ran for the cover of the trees. Behind
her she heard the echo of the doorbell seemingly thundering through the flat and she felt
sick, grateful that she had run rather than
taking the risk of hanging back to face Percy

again. She didn't owe him that courtesy. If he had felt violent the night before he would feel even more violent when she told him she wasn't coming to the church. And no man was *ever* going to hit her again!

'Something's set off one of the motion sensors on the fence,' Ruy's security phoned to inform him. 'It's probably an animal but it would be safest if you stayed indoors, sir, and let us handle this.'

Reflecting on the state-of-the-art security he had originally set up to ensure his privacy rather than his personal security, Ruy almost rolled his eyes. He had not wanted security of any kind with him, but so successful had he become in his role at Valiente Capital that his insurers now wanted him protected everywhere he went. He had been forced to build the necessary accommodation for bodyguards even though in his opinion the chances of a kidnapping deep in the wilds of Norfolk, where he was entirely unknown, were extremely low.

'It's fine. I'll handle it myself,' he imparted before dealing with the polite attempt to argue that inevitably followed.

He slung on a thick coat and scarf because the temperature had dropped radically once it began snowing. Snow and it was almost May, he reflected in wonderment; what a barbarous climate that could go from spring one day back to winter the next! He had bought hundreds of acres of woodland with the house and had surrounded it with an impenetrable security fence. Reflecting on the peaceful beauty of his surroundings with satisfaction, he jumped into his four-wheel drive and drove down the track into the woods, parking a few minutes later to get out and stride through the trees to head for the west sector of the fence, which lay nearest the village.

Trapped in the dilapidated tree house, Suzy shivered violently. She didn't know where her wits had been when she had run off into the trees. She could have done with the knowledge in advance that someone had mysteriously cut the woods in half with a giant metal fence, which meant that it was no longer possible to reach the main road on the other side of them. Getting over the fence had entailed climbing a tree and jumping and, in that mad panic that had gripped her where only adrenalin ruled, she had managed those actions fine even if the dress was the worse for wear as a result. The snow coming on had persuaded her to head for the old tree house to take shelter for a while.

And then everything else that could go wrong *had* gone wrong. The tree house she remembered from childhood had lost its roof long ago and offered no shelter whatsoever. She had only just managed to make it up onto the platform when the ladder, which had cracked under her weight, fell and smashed to pieces. Now she was stuck until she had gathered the energy to climb back down the tree, but she was horribly cold and she no longer trusted her arms and legs to keep her safe. Worse still, it hadn't even occurred to her to snatch up her phone when she ran and, dazed with physical misery and aches and pains, she was feeling very sorry for herself even while she wondered vaguely why she wasn't more actively concerned about her predicament.

Ruy walked along the fence and found the obstruction. It was a branch, he assumed until he reached it and saw that it was the remains of a very roughly put-together ladder. He tossed it away from the fence.

'It *would* have to be you,' a woman's voice pronounced in a tone of loathing. 'Just my luck.'

Startled when he had believed himself utterly alone, Ruy swung round and glanced up in sheer disbelief at the woman swinging her boot-clad legs on the edge of a tumbledown wooden structure that he had not even known existed in his woods. A tree house, he realised, or at least the remains of one, something he had craved as a child but had never been allowed to have.

'Is this the part where I say, "Rapunzel… Rapunzel…let down your hair"?'

'You're *not* my prince!' Suzy hurled at him accusingly, not in the mood for a fairy-tale allusion. 'But you can still get me down from this blasted tree!'

'*Sí*, Your Highness,' Ruy countered with appreciation at such rudeness and the novelty of it. 'The use of the word please might be sensible in the circumstances.'

'You've got smartass written all over you!' Suzy raged down at him incredulously.

'I'm stuck… I'm freezing and it's snowing. So, please, please, *please*!'

Ruy stared up at her, dark-as-pitch eyes narrowing in disbelief and flaring gold as he registered the veil fluttering into view behind her fall of copper spiral curls. 'Are you wearing a wedding dress?' he almost whispered.

'Are you going to help me get down from here? Or are you planning to keep on asking me stupid questions until I'm a frozen corpse?' Suzy snarled, her tongue stumbling round the words and slurring the syllables.

Involuntarily, Ruy grinned. 'You're not that far from the ground. Jump down and I'll catch you,' he told her.

'And you're *smiling* at seeing me in this

condition!' Suzy framed, almost incandescent with fury at such stupidity while she wondered why she could no longer speak properly. 'Don't you recognise an emergency?'

All that passion fired her eyes to green-glass brilliance in her pale little face. His fingers itching for a stick of charcoal and a blank page, he studied her with the fierce enchantment of a born artist and walked beneath the tree house. 'Just push yourself over the edge and fall,' he instructed.

'I'm scared of heights, you dummy!' Suzy launched.

'So close your eyes and trust me,' Ruy advised without sympathy, 'while you're telling me how you got over my fence.'

'*Your* fence…should've guessed. I climbed a tree and jumped down.'

'I thought you were too scared of heights,' Ruy pointed out, since she had yet to move an inch.

'I was running on adrenalin just then,' she mumbled shakily, and he regretted mentioning the height because he had already noticed the shivering and the slurring of her speech and the pale colour of her lips and he suspected she was suffering from hypothermia.

'You've left him at the altar...haven't you?' Ruy gathered harshly, keen to distract her because she was shaking so badly without seeming to be aware of it that he was beginning to appreciate that she could also be deep in some kind of shock.

She nodded her head jerkily in silence.

'Not a very kind thing to do,' Ruy dared.

'How dare you?' Suzy shot as hotly at him as he had hoped, and she slid off the edge of the platform and down into his arms.

Ruy staggered as he caught her because of the force of her fall but she was a slight weight, a small, curvy shape that smelled of oranges and sunshine. Weird, he thought, abstractedly drinking in the scent of her hair, liking it in some even weirder way. 'I just wanted you down from the tree as fast as possible,' he murmured soothingly as he tried to put her down again. 'Winding you up seems to work a treat.'

Her legs buckled and he told her to lean against him while he removed his coat and wrapped it round her before lifting her again.

'I don't know why you wind me up so much...well, actually I do,' Suzy muttered jaggedly, from the depths of his giant warmly lined jacket. 'If you hadn't been in the bar last night talking to me, it wouldn't have happened...but maybe I'm lucky it happened because I had no idea he would do what he did, so maybe I should be thanking you instead of thinking it was all your fault because *he* thought you were flirting with me.'

'How was it my fault? And what did happen?' Ruy pressed, strong arms closed firmly round her and making her feel oddly safe for the first time after long hours of agonising while she had lain sleepless throughout the night.

'Nothing...nothing happened,' she muttered, struggling to concentrate.

In the stark harshness of the spring light, Ruy looked down at her and registered the bruise on her cheekbone and the reddening and hint of swelling round her little nose. 'He *hit* you? That's why you left him standing?' he demanded rawly.

'Let's not talk about it. And then he arrived early at the church… I saw him from the window,' she admitted unevenly. 'He came over to the flat and Dad was out and I just panicked because I couldn't face him again. I knew he would pile on the pressure and make threats. He knew what he had done, and he wanted to make sure I would go through with the wedding. He'll be in a towering rage with me now and I didn't want to risk that confrontation.'

'Cabrón!' Ruy bit out the insult in Spanish, settling her carefully into the passenger seat of his vehicle and tugging out his phone to ring his sister for advice; as a GP, she was generally home at weekends. He spoke to her in French because Cecile's mother had been French, and he didn't want to take the chance that Suzy might understand what he was saying. Cecile was shocked and told him what

to do best for Suzy while promising to call round to check her over.

'Shouldn't we be contacting the police to report the assault?' Ruy prompted as he turned the car.

'No...*no*!' From the depths of his coat, Suzy shot him a look of pure horror. 'It would only make Percy more vindictive and I can't afford to do that.'

'We'll see,' Ruy said lightly, although he had no intention of standing back while the abuser got off scot-free because he had literally terrorised his victim into such fear that she couldn't currently see the situation as it was. He wanted more information but knew it was unfair to press her when she was in a weakened state of confusion. He was also experiencing an extremely strong urge to protect her from further harm.

'He has a lot of power,' she mumbled thickly. 'You can't afford to antagonise people like that.'

Ruy was outraged by the depth of her fear of a small-time local businessman. It was the strangest feeling. He could not recall ever being so angry about anything that did not directly affect him. After all, he did not get involved in other people's problems. On the one occasion when he had abandoned that rule years earlier the situation had blown up in his face when, by trying to help, he had simply done more damage, or so it had seemed. But Suzy was different, he told himself soothingly, because he had no personal or sexual interest in her. She wasn't his type, absolutely *not* his type. Ruy was drawn to quietly spoken brunettes, not short, curvy redheads with sharp tongues.

'Gosh, I'm so sleepy,' she whispered through chattering teeth.

'You can't go to sleep, not yet anyway,' Ruy responded, ramming the vehicle to a halt in front of his property and racing round to the passenger side to lift her out at speed.

He strode up the stairs to the bathroom off the bedroom and laid her down with care on the floor. 'You need to get undressed. You have to get out of your wet clothes,' he told her as he rang his housekeeper to order a drink and a snack for her.

'So you can paint me?' Suzy asked with a giggle, entirely removed from the urgency of her condition.

'Not just yet,' Ruy countered, crouching down to extract her from his coat and unpinning the wilted veil with ease to toss it aside. 'How the hell do I get you out of this dress?'

'H-hooks!' Suzy advised with another inappropriate giggle.

Suppressing a groan, seeing by the state of her pale bluish hands that there was no way she was capable of undressing herself, Ruy gently bent her over and embarked on the many hooks. His wide sensual mouth clamped down in a hard line as the bruises began to appear. Against her naturally pale skin purple fingerprints ornamented her slim shoulders and upper arms while a long painful scrape and bruising marred her slender spine. He knew he wanted to find the guy responsible and thump him hard where it hurt most. The knowledge shook him because Ruy was very controlled and disciplined and he virtually never gave way to emotional reactions. After all, he had spent his entire life suppressing natural inclinations to concentrate on what he saw as his duty.

He stalked into his bedroom to dig a tee shirt out of a drawer. After his conversation with his sister, he was wondering if Suzy had been sexually assaulted as well and he felt murderous as he dropped the tee shirt over her down-bent head and threaded her limp arms through the holes before propping her up. Suzy was still shivering violently, mumbling to herself, barely aware, it seemed, of her surroundings or of him. That was a novel experience for a man used to being treated like a billionaire trophy to be acquired at any cost. Lifting her up with ease, he carried her into his bedroom, laid her down and rolled her into the soft blanket he had laid out, finally settling her back against the carved headboard like a cocoon.

'Now you eat and drink,' Ruy announced.

'Not hungry,' she muttered.

He wasn't listening because Cecile had given him his instructions and he would follow them to the letter.

'A hot bath would have warmed me up,' Suzy complained.

'Your body temperature has to be restored slowly,' Ruy contradicted. 'It's safer that way. It would have hurt like hell anyway if I'd plunged you into a hot bath.'

'It...*would*?' Her head fell back against the headboard. 'Where am I?'

'My house.'

'How did I get here?'

'It's not important. What's your fiancé's name?'

Suzy stiffened, drooping eyelids lifting high on her wide green eyes. 'Percy Brenton.'

Percy Brenton, you are toast, Ruy reflected with satisfaction at acquiring the name. 'Why were you marrying him?'

'Dad...' Her voice faltered and she blinked rapidly. 'That's private, I can't discuss that.'

'You can discuss it with me. It will remain confidential. You have been harmed. I will not harm you in any way,' Ruy informed her levelly, his sheer confidence leaping out at her in his stance, his tone, his bright golden eyes that were no longer darker than pitch. Gorgeous eyes, she thought absently, totally gorgeous, exotic eyes.

A knock sounded on a door somewhere and her eyes slid off him to bump up against un-familiar views and the huge window over-looking the snowy woodland scene outside. It was raining now, and the unseasonal fall of light snow was already melting fast. She was disorientated because she had never been in such a big bedroom or seen such furniture or the kind of classic paintings ornamenting the rough stone walls. It looked incredibly opu-lent and that was quite outside her experience.

Ruy stalked back into view with a tray. He sank down on the edge of the bed and ex-tended a glass in a metal holder to her.

'Not thirsty,' she admitted.

Ruy ignored her, raising the glass to her lips. 'Drink,' he urged.

'You're very bossy.' She sighed, sipping with difficulty and grimacing. 'What is it?'

'Milk and honey—'

'Brandy would have been nicer,' she told him, settling her dilated gaze on his and internally swooning, not from the sweetness of the drink, but from the sheer carnal impact of those lean bronzed features and the dark golden eyes so intent on hers. He packed a real punch in the charisma stakes, and he had the most amazing long black curling lashes fringing his eyes, the sort a woman would have killed to have.

'You're not allowed alcohol... Cecile's orders,' Ruy told her apologetically.

'Your sister's really nice,' she told him lamely.

'And I'm not?' Ruy grinned, having caught the unspoken comparison.

'You're just very...forceful,' Suzy framed.

'Don't you dare compare me to *him*!' Ruy warned in a husky undertone and something about that tone, something about that smouldering dark golden appraisal, set a fire alight in her pelvis and, without even thinking about it, Suzy leant forward and pressed her parted lips against his.

And for a split second he froze, and she thought, *I've got it wrong,* along with, *What the heck am I doing?* as astonishment at her aberrant invitation rippled through her. But that was before he responded, a lean hand coming up to cup her nape and tip her head up and he was kissing her back and it was *amazing,* literally the most electrifying kiss she had ever had. The firm seal of his sensual lips against hers, the delving exploration of his tongue, the very taste of him were overwhelming.

He jerked back from her with such abruptness that she was startled. 'I'm sorry,' he said flatly. 'That shouldn't have happened. You are not yourself right now.'

'I don't know what you're talking about,' she began, her face burning hot with mortification because she, unbelievable as it was to her at that moment, had made the first move.

Ruy rested the plate with the sandwich down on her lap. 'Eat…it'll help.'

At that point, Suzy wanted to sink through a hole in the mattress rather than try to eat. Her brain felt as if it were in a swamp. She remembered the attraction but not why or how she had succumbed to it. Her body was warming up now, indeed she was nearly too warm, and her hands came up from under the blanket to push it down and free her fingers. Like a drowning swimmer, she snatched at a sandwich as though it were a lifebelt.

Ruy was standing circumspectly now by the side of the bed. 'You're confused right now.'

Suzy nodded. Whether she liked it or not, it was sadly true because her brain cells still felt as though they had been plunged into sludge.

Striving to breathe less audibly, Ruy swung away to the window, fiercely aroused, not wanting her to notice the tight fit of his black jeans at the groin. He didn't know what had happened either. That conflagration of passion had come at him out of the blue and he didn't like that, he specifically didn't want *any* woman to have that much of an effect on him. It was too risky; it didn't fit into his life plan in which everything was to be in moderation. No wild passion, no fierce sympathy, no anything that made him feel vulnerable or out of control, because that path could lead to devastation and guilty regret and he was determined never to revisit such unnecessary and dangerous feelings again.

The urgent knock at the door sent his head twisting round, gratitude flaring at the awareness that his sister must have arrived, a welcome interruption indeed to the tense atmosphere that was forming.

'That will be Cecile. I'll bring her in, leave you to it,' Ruy intoned with a relief he couldn't conceal.

Mortified beyond bearing, Suzy lowered her head and cringed inside herself for the mistake she had made.

CHAPTER THREE

CECILE WAS BRISK and kind, the very best she could have been in such circumstances. She gently insisted on documenting and photographing Suzy's abrasions, informing her that it was a matter of legal procedure.

'But I don't want the police involved,' Suzy proclaimed.

'Have you really thought that through? Has it occurred to you that he has probably done this sort of stuff before and got away with it? Or that if you don't make a complaint, some other woman after you will suffer the same as you are now? It could have been much *worse* for you, Suzy…and he could come after you again.'

All those sensible points got through to Suzy and made her squirm and feel sick and ashamed and frightened, because Percy's attitude *had* given her the impression that she was not the first woman that he had attacked. 'I know it could have been worse…look, I'll think about it,' she muttered uneasily.

'Obviously what you do is up to you,' Cecile conceded gently. 'For now, I recommend that you have a nap, because you look exhausted.'

'I'd love a shower first… I don't suppose—' Her voice ran out as the other woman helpfully tugged open a door on the other side of the room.

Alone, Suzy crept barefoot into the fanciest bathroom she had ever seen outside a magazine. Natural stone with veins of quartz that glimmered like gold covered the floor and the walls and provided a massive shower, while the bath sat up a short flight of steps by the window and looked very much like the sort of backdrop a film star might have used. Eyes wide, Suzy peeled off her clothing, picking up the pitiful roll of banknotes she had thrust into her bra earlier that day. She glowered at her own reflection, seeing the shadows beneath her eyes and the ugly bruising on her body before turning away from the view and switching on the shower.

Downstairs, Cecile surveyed her younger brother. 'I know you must want your peace back. I suppose you want me to take her out of here for you,' she assumed. 'She doesn't want to go home yet because of the bruises.'

'No. I want her to stay.'

'*Stay?* But where are you planning to put her?' the vivacious brunette asked in surprise. 'You haven't got a spare room.'

Put on the spot while cursing his stubborn refusal to consider extending the house when he had bought it , Ruy shrugged a broad shoulder with something less than his usual cool. 'I'll sort something out. I have the studio. I'll buy a bed. I want her to stay because I want to paint her.'

'You want to...*paint* her?' Cecile shook her dark head in visible disbelief. 'Right now, she needs support and understanding, not some guy who just wants to use her in some other way!'

'I have no plans to use her in *any* way,' Ruy retorted drily.

'I'm sorry, but seeing her like that upset me. She's such a kind girl and usually so lively.' His sister sighed. 'I think that awful man, Brenton, must have some kind of nasty hold on her because I can't understand why she's reluctant to report him to the police. I bet it's something to do with money. Ever since we moved here I've heard rumours that the pub is going bust.'

Ruy tensed, his hard, expressive mouth compressing. 'May I ask if—?'

'No, you can't ask me anything confidential about a patient and you should know better!' Cecile told him firmly. 'Now, tell me, have you accepted the invitation to our brother's wedding yet?'

Ruy grimaced. 'Not yet. Had he extended the invite to you and Charles as well I would have accepted immediately.'

'Rodrigo isn't prepared to recognise me as

a sibling yet. He's a complete snob,' Cecile commented with the dry amusement of indifference on that score. 'I'm just grateful he has a twin who isn't. I think you should give him a second chance, Ruy, and trust that there will be no unpleasantness this time.'

Ruy said nothing. The history of what Cecile called unpleasantness between the brothers had begun when they were children and eight years earlier had significantly worsened to the extent that the brothers no longer spoke at all. He refused to think about the murky secret in their past, the reason behind that complete breakdown in communication. Yet that was why Ruy had been astonished by the wedding invite and he was as reluctant to refuse it and cause offence as he was to attend and risk an angry scene.

What he really needed, he reflected uneasily, was a female companion to act as a buffer between him and his brother and his bride, but any woman of his acquaintance whom he invited to accompany him to a family wedding would immediately assume that their relationship was more meaningful than it was. That was a hassle he didn't need but it made him think of Suzy again, Suzy who struck him as more a wild and free young woman than a conventional conservative one. Someone like her would make the perfect companion. She would be different enough to intrigue his relatives and his brother but too young and restless to harbour any serious expectations of him afterwards.

A couple of hours later, Suzy stirred and awakened, stretching with a wince because pushing her head into the pillow ensured she felt the tender swelling on the back of it. Cecile had tried to persuade her to go for a hospital scan, but Suzy was confident that it was simply a painful bump. She lay there picturing the guests who must have turned up for her wedding and their incredulity over her non-appearance and she flinched, wiping her mind free of the embarrassing images again. What was done was done, she told herself, and she could not regret backing out of her agreement with Percy.

She had returned to bed with her wet hair wrapped in a towel and it took inventiveness to make herself even vaguely presentable because her curls had gone crazy. She finger-sorted and flattened and dampened and gave up in the end, glancing in the mirror and frowning before putting on her biker boots again and leaving the room.

Emerging onto a landing she didn't even recall seeing before, she headed for the stairs since there didn't appear to be anywhere else to go.

Ruy looked up from his sketch pad and saw her on the stairs, long pale, shapely legs thrust into those ridiculous boots, his capacious tee shirt almost hanging off one slender white shoulder. Her hair was wild and untamed, a messy mass of curls surrounding her triangular face in a cloud of Titian glory, huge green eyes striking his. He was entranced and he knew it, *knew* it was the artist in him, not the man, because for the first time in her presence he hadn't got hard.

'Ruy,' she said, awkward in the buzzing silence, her attention falling to the slew of discarded sketches littering the coffee table and squinting at the nearest image, involuntarily impressed by the few slashing strokes on the page, which even she registered as recognisable. 'Have you been drawing me?'

Ruy tossed the pad down on the coffee table, the faintest colour defining his remarkable cheekbones, dark eyes flaring gold as ingots as he looked up at her.

'You look *so* guilty!' Suzy carolled in unexpected delight, a teasing grin forming on her lips as she settled down on a capacious sofa and curled up. 'You *know* you should have asked permission first.'

Unaccustomed to being read that accurately, Ruy suppressed a sardonic retort because she was smiling, and then the entirety of his attention was stolen by a glimpse of slender inner thigh that sent a pulse thrumming directly to his groin. It was that flawless skin of hers, so translucent and smooth that he could only wonder how it would feel beneath his fingertips. 'I should have done,' he agreed in a driven undertone, averting his gaze and willing his hormones to stop derailing him, disconcerted that she could make him react with so adolescent a lack of restraint. 'But occasionally the desire to draw pushes me beyond the limits of courtesy. I apologise.'

'You don't need to,' Suzy told him immediately, wondering why his admission that the pull of his art tempted him into forgetting his manners should strike her as so very, very sexy. She didn't think like that, at least, she never had before meeting him. It was downright unnerving, in the wake of that first kiss initiated by her, to appreciate that around him she *still* didn't seem capable of behaving normally. 'You helped me today and I won't forget that.'

'I could scarcely have abandoned you in the tree house,' Ruy pointed out. 'That would have been manslaughter at the very least.'

And there it was: that *other* side of his nature, Suzy labelled straight away, that very controlled, pretty arrogant and almost chilling attitude of detachment that had set her on edge at their first meeting. 'Never mind. I owe you a few sketches,' she told him dismissively.

'What I would *really* like is some clarification on the score of the wedding that misfired,' Ruy admitted as he slid fluidly upright. 'We'll talk over dinner, which should be ready in a few minutes...'

'Oh...' Suzy said uncertainly, his sheer confidence that she would choose to confide in him leaving her bemused. 'Can I help?'

'I have a housekeeper. She does the catering.' Ruy thrust open a door into a dining room with a contemporary glass table that was already set with cloth napkins, crystal glasses and gleaming cutlery.

Intimidated by that very formal setting, Suzy quickly dropped down into the chair he had tugged out for her. 'Did you build this house? I didn't even know it existed and yet it can't be much more than a mile from the village.'

'No, I bought it as is. The original owner of the property was something in showbusiness and this was to be his retirement home, but he passed away before he could move in,' Ruy explained.

'It's a beautiful house,' Suzy remarked, a little more relaxed by the assumption that Ruy was not personally responsible for the profound luxury of their surroundings. The property wasn't in a fashionable area and although the rooms were very spacious there didn't seem to be that many of them. The house was a quirky one-off, so possibly he had got it cheap, she reasoned. On the other hand, equally possibly, he was a very successful artist. How would she know? That she had not recognised his name meant nothing because she had no knowledge of the art world.

'The woods sold it for me more than anything else,' Ruy told her. 'Now, some things you said earlier today have worried me and I can't pretend you didn't say them. You said

Brenton had too much power and that he would pile on the pressure and threaten you. Aside from the assault, why are you so frightened of the man?'

Suzy flushed from cheek to temple, the heat of mortification engulfing her in a tide, for she hadn't realised just how much she had revealed while she was in the grip of hypothermia. 'I'm sorry, I can't discuss that.'

Undaunted, Ruy stretched his big powerful body back into his seat and lifted his dark head high, narrowed dark eyes of astonishing intensity locked to her. 'Does it relate to your father's ownership of the village pub?' he enquired smoothly. 'I've already learned that Brenton has a reputation for unscrupulous behaviour and that his financial dealings may be questionable.'

Hugely disconcerted by that statement, Suzy was grateful when the door opened and an older woman bustled in with plates. The interruption was welcome but at the same time Suzy was desperate to know how Ruy had acquired such information, bearing in mind that she had lived in the area all her life and had not heard so much as a whisper of such rumours.

'Who told you that about Percy?' she pressed as soon as they were alone again.

'When I make financial enquiries, I have good sources.' Ruy shook out his napkin with infuriating cool. 'Let us enjoy our meal.'

Fizzing with frustration, Suzy settled her attention on her tomato and mozzarella first course and ate with an appetite that surprised her. Only when she thought about it did she recall that she had skipped her evening meal the night before and breakfast that morning and had only had the sandwich that Ruy had given her. Yet it felt to her as though weeks had passed since the previous day, because the future she had expected had suddenly vanished and she had no idea what would take the place of her acting as Percy's wife. She supposed that after they had lost the pub she and her father would move to the nearest town in search of employment.

The main course, another sophisticated

dish, arrived and Ruy offered her wine with the quip that Cecile wasn't present to police her.

'I've still got a bit of a headache and I took painkillers, so no, thanks, for the moment.'

'Now,' Ruy breathed with blistering assurance. 'Enlighten me about your father's financial dealings with your ex.'

'How on earth do you even *know* that he has dealings?' Suzy exclaimed, dropping her knife and fork with a clatter to emphasise her annoyance.

'I refuse to believe that love had anything to do with your planned marriage to Brenton,' Ruy intoned drily. 'By nature, he's a thug and a bully.'

'You only met him for about ten seconds!' Suzy snatched at her glass of water to occupy her restless hands, unnerved by Ruy's steady stubborn persistence. 'How could you even know that?'

A grim light shadowed Ruy's gaze at that question. Being raised by a bully had made it very easy for him to recognise the warning signs. He had not had a pleasant child-hood but, in many ways, his more sensitive twin brother, unable to handle their father's lacerating tongue, had suffered much more in failing to meet the standards that Armando Valiente demanded.

'Just tell me the truth, because you *have* to confide in someone.'

'No, I don't.' Suzy sucked in a ragged breath and picked up her cutlery again with determination.

'And you have to stop being scared for long enough to go to the police,' Ruy contended.

Colour flooded the pallor that had spread across her small stiff face. 'I want to go to the police…but I daren't do it,' she muttered shakily.

'Tell me why not,' Ruy prodded afresh.

And a tempestuous mixture of desperation and resentment assailed Suzy. Green eyes flashed with defensiveness and she lifted her chin as though daring him to judge her. 'Dad borrowed from the bank to update the bar but we didn't do enough business to keep up the loan. When Dad was threatened with repossession, Percy stepped in. The old loan was repaid and Percy extended a new one with lower payments.'

'How did you become involved in that arrangement?' Ruy enquired, resting back in his chair with his wine glass elegantly cradled in one lean brown hand, so stunningly handsome in that moment that she momentarily lost the thread of the dialogue. As she gazed almost blankly back at him, her mouth dry, her pelvis thrumming with the strangest pulse that made her thighs twitch and tense, he had to repeat the question.

'I wasn't involved until six months ago,' Suzy admitted in a rueful rush. 'Then Percy said he'd write the loan off if I married him and that if I *didn't* marry him he would take the pub off Dad. After a couple of discussions, I agreed but I… I told him I wouldn't have sex with him. I would be his wife in all other ways though and nobody else would know the truth of our relationship,' she completed with scarlet cheeks.

'*Dios mio*...and he *agreed* to that?' Ruy marvelled.

Suzy nodded miserably. 'But I'm not sure now that he planned to stick to the rules and that he didn't start hating me for them.'

'How much does your father know about Brenton's blackmail?'

At that question, Suzy frowned. 'He knows nothing about any of it! Dad would never have agreed to let me marry Percy for his benefit.'

'And the loan outstanding amounts to fifty thousand pounds or so?' Ruy queried, startling her with his accuracy and, when he met her troubled gaze, dealing her an eloquent smile. 'That *was* why you plucked that particular sum out of the air, wasn't it?'

'A ridiculous amount,' she mumbled in severe chagrin as she recalled that conversation in the bar when he had urged her to name her price for modelling for him. 'I wasn't serious, of course...you do know that, don't you? I'm truly not a greedy person. It's just, Percy was starting to scare me, and I'd pretty much do anything for my dad.'

'That's not a sin. It's proof of loyalty and of your love for a parent. You were willing to make a sacrifice to protect your father.'

'But I tumbled at the last fence and now I've just dug Dad into a deeper hole!' Suzy argued with a guilt-ridden shake of her head. 'Now, after being left at the altar, Percy will be out for blood.'

'He's already had as much blood as he's getting and he's not taking any more out of your particular hide,' Ruy asserted with scorching conviction. 'Surely you realise that Brenton will now want to approach you with some suggestion aimed at saving his own skin? If you choose to prosecute him for assault his reputation will be ruined. He may well offer to write off that loan in an effort to keep you quiet.'

Suzy's eyes widened. 'No way would he do that. Percy has the reputation for collecting on all his debts.'

'You have to report him to the police,' Ruy continued. 'And I can offer you a way to do that that will protect you *and* your father's business.'

'I'm not a kid, Ruy. There's no magic fix for this mess,' Suzy told him heavily as she pushed her plate away. 'And in many ways, it's a mess of my own making. I was stupidly trusting. I should never have agreed to marry Percy in the first place. That wretched money seemed to give him the impression that he was buying me body and soul and that that deprived me of any right to respect or decency. What I agreed to was wrong, though, and perhaps I deserve what happened.'

'*Valgame Dios!* Of course, you didn't *deserve* it!' Ruy argued in heated dissent.

'And now you're talking about making me an offer…presumably money,' Suzy gathered with a little moue of distaste and a look of reproach in his direction that made him seal his wide, sensual mouth shut again. 'Please… *don't*. I'll think over the idea of modelling for you, but I don't know how it could be organised now because Dad and I will probably be leaving the village soon. But please,

please, do *not* try to buy me like Percy did… I've learned my lesson and I'm off the market now.'

Unusual frustration currented through Ruy, but he was adept at steering paths round obstacles and varying his approach. Being flexible, innovative and highly intelligent had made him a living legend in the financial world and he recognised that Suzy would naturally be highly resistant to any offer of cash assistance after the experience she'd had at Brenton's hands. The germ of an idea struck Ruy and at first he rejected it, deeming it not to be his place to interfere in a family matter or, indeed, in a family business. Even so, as he ran the concept swiftly through his brain he saw *how* he could extend his help without making Suzy feel that he had bribed, bought or blackmailed her. And how he too would benefit from the arrangement beyond her modelling for him. He would ask her to accompany him to his brother's wedding.

Even so, his most pressing concern should be protecting Suzy from her ex, shouldn't it? His thoughts froze on that startling point. Exactly when had he developed that strange notion? When had he last become this involved in problems that were not his to solve? He wanted to paint Suzy, which put her in an entirely different category, he assured himself. Having shaken off his unease over that uncharacteristic urge to protect, Ruy found that he could think with clarity again. To ensure Suzy's security from further threats, or indeed dodgy proposals, he would need to view first-hand the loan agreement her father had signed. Once that problem was settled, he would consider his own needs and wishes, proving that he was *not* the selfish bastard his sister had implied, he reasoned with satisfaction, his momentary tension evaporating.

'So, what sort of stuff do you paint?' Suzy asked.

'People, mainly portraits, usually women.'

'Nudes?' Suzy suddenly prompted in a slightly strangled voice.

'I have done, but generally my models remain clothed,' Ruy responded with a glint of amusement in his gaze, because she was shifting in her seat like an embarrassed child, her dismay at the prospect of posing nude for him clear as day. A prickle of interest in seeing those pale luscious curves unveiled shimmied through him like a sudden shot of some dangerously addictive drug. Taken aback by that loss of artistic objectivity, he struggled to suppress that leap of desire, all amusement buried by his own far too personal response.

Dessert was served as Suzy confessed, 'I know nothing about art.'

'Why would you when it's not an interest of yours?' Keen to stick strictly to business as he saw it, Ruy added, 'If you agreed to model for me, you would have to first sign a non-disclosure agreement, which would prevent you from mentioning my name or indeed any details about me. It's a standard safeguard I use with every model I employ.'

'Why would you do that?' Suzy surveyed him, eyes as green and fresh as spring leaves wide with curiosity and surprise. 'Don't artists need publicity to boost their careers and the prices their work commands?'

'Privacy is more important to me,' Ruy said quietly.

Suzy waved an expressive hand at the elegant table and her surroundings and laughed. '*And*, it doesn't look like you're hurting for a spare penny or two!' she teased.

It was that playful quality, which his sister had called liveliness, that appealed to him, Ruy decided, his attention locking to that full pink lower lip, recalling the taste of her, the taste of temptation. When she smiled she practically lit up the room. Yet when she had danced, even before he had seen her face, he had wanted to capture her in oils, to somehow magically meld her innate grace of movement into the painting. Obviously, there would have to be more than one canvas, he conceded, to capture her different moods.

'I would like you to consider granting me another favour,' he divulged.

On the brink of asking why she would consider doing him any favours, Suzy caught her tongue between her teeth, recalling how supportive he had been.

'I have to attend my brother's wedding in a couple of weeks and it would be easier if I had a woman with me, a woman willing to pretend that she was engaged to me.'

'Why on earth would you want that?' she exclaimed, too disconcerted to guard her tongue.

'I have a troubled relationship with my brother. My presence at his wedding would be smoother if he were to believe that I had found a woman of my own,' Ruy revealed reluctantly.

'Very strange...and not for me,' Suzy said ruefully. 'I was Percy's fake bride and it didn't work out well for me. I don't want to be faking anything for anyone now.'

'Consider it. I think it would suit you right now to escape the local gossip for a while. The wedding is in Spain.'

'Spain!' Suzy rolled her eyes as though he had suggested the moon as a destination, but the reference to local gossip made her grimace. It annoyed her that he was right once again. Leaving the village even for a few days was a welcome idea, particularly as it would put her out of reach of Percy, she acknowledged. 'But, I'll think about it.'

Smothering a yawn over coffee, Suzy began to droop, the events of the past few days catching up with her again. Ruy urged her to have an early night.

'I shouldn't still be here,' Suzy registered abruptly, absently amazed by the way she had simply taken Ruy Rivera's hospitality for granted. 'I should go home.'

'Where were you heading when you went into the woods?'

'I had a vague notion of hitching a lift to the railway station. Can you imagine it? Me in that wedding dress and probably not even having enough money to buy a train ticket...' She shook her head and sighed. 'I'm sorry I involved you in all this.'

'You're welcome to stay. At least here, you are out of Brenton's reach,' Ruy pointed out sneakily.

'And it's handy to keep me around if you want to paint me.' Suzy's bright gaze glimmered with humour. 'I've got your measure, Mr Rivera…you will never be slow to take advantage of a useful opportunity.'

Ruy's rare grin slashed his expressive mouth, his dark eyes flashing gold with appreciation at the intelligence sparkling in her appraisal. 'Exactly,' he agreed.

Suzy paused at the foot of the stairs and glanced back at him, her delicate profile and the scattering of freckles on the bridge of her nose as fascinating to him as the fragile white shoulder poking through her spiralling auburn curls. 'Thanks for helping me today. The wedding thing sounds challenging, I'm afraid, and I don't think I fancy trying it. I'll do the model thing for you, though, as long as I can keep my clothes on,' she announced with a gauche bluntness that almost made Ruy laugh out loud.

Involuntarily he was entranced by that kind of modesty. Was it an act? Understandably, he was suspicious. After all, the majority of women Ruy met couldn't wait to get their clothes *off* for his benefit, be it as a model in the studio or as a one-night stand. And then there were the unwelcome invitations like the maid who had sashayed into his bedroom with his breakfast one morning naked as a jaybird, or the PA who had just stripped off down to her fancy lingerie on the first and last day of her employment with him.

'I'll see you in the morning.'

'Ah…' Ruy shifted a fluid hand. 'Would it be possible for me to first remove some clothes from the bedroom?'

On the stairs, Suzy froze and whipped round. 'It's *your* bedroom? I'm putting you out of your own bed? Oh, that won't do at all! I'll sleep on one of the sofas.'

'That's not necessary,' Ruy declared, striding up to crowd her on the stairs and with his very height and breadth somehow persuading her to move on up to the landing.

'*But—?*'

'I'm sleeping in my studio,' Ruy countered firmly, having already procured a bed for his use. 'When I bought this place it was a ground-floor bedroom.'

Suzy hovered uncomfortably as Ruy removed items from drawers and a closet and returned to her side.

'I'm going out tonight. I wouldn't want to disturb you when I return,' Ruy murmured softly, scorching dark golden eyes welded to her.

Suzy was bright pink with self-consciousness, the sort of deep dire self-consciousness that she had suffered as a schoolgirl. 'It just doesn't seem right, me putting you out.'

Ruy rested a long brown forefinger gently across her parted lips. '*Silencio, por favor…* it is nothing.'

Her lips prickled even below that light touch and her pupils dilated. 'Ruy—'

'It is very sexy that you *didn't* suggest that I share the bed with you,' Ruy murmured softly, gazing down at her for all the world as though that omission on her part were an act of astonishing restraint.

Thoroughly taken aback, Suzy shot the vast

bed a glance, acknowledging that it was large enough to absorb two couples, never mind one, but she was still struggling to get her head around the telling fact that he found her failure to ask him to join her in the bed sexier than an invitation would have been. And that concept lay so far beyond her grasp of the male outlook on sex that she could only gaze back at him in incredulity at the comment.

'Sleep well, *buenas noches*,' Ruy husked, striding out and leaving her standing there in a fog of confusion.

Did Ruy get women coming on to him so often that it had become the norm for him? He was extraordinarily good-looking, she conceded thoughtfully, picturing that lean, strong, sculpted face and those stunning eyes that could go from dark to smouldering gold. Very, very good-looking, she concluded as she made use of the new toothbrush laid out for her and prepared for bed. She had studied him throughout their meal, seeking a flaw, nonplussed to be unable to find one. Those gorgeous looks of his had briefly mesmerised her into stealing that kiss. She winced for herself afresh. Talk about making a production out of being attracted to a guy! She had practically shouted it in his face. But she was comforted by the conviction that most women probably found Ruy Rivera extremely appealing and he was clearly used to it and bored by it, so her foolish little kiss would soon be forgotten.

As she would soon forget him, once he was out of her radius, she told herself soothingly. She was a very down-to-earth and sensible woman, always had been, always would be. Accepting Percy's offer had been a mistake, a glitch caused by panic on her father's behalf. She felt quite nervous and sick at the thought of what her rearranged future might now hold for her and her father, but she was well used to making the best of what she got in life even if it often wasn't what she wanted or felt she needed. And she would handle whatever happened, she told herself squarely, slipping into the gloriously comfortable bed.

As Suzy drifted inexorably into the deep

sleep of emotional exhaustion, Ruy was striding into the village pub to introduce himself to her father. No sooner had he intimated that he had news of Suzy than the barmaid was left in charge and he was ushered into a private room where he sat down to discuss business over a revered Scottish malt while thinking that Suzy might try to object but he *was* sticking strictly to the guidelines she had given him…

CHAPTER FOUR

SUZY SLEPT IN and scrambled out of bed in a rush to head into the bathroom, stumbling to a halt when she saw clothing lying across the chair by the wall, clothing that was familiar. She stared in frowning puzzlement at a pair of her own skinny jeans, her favourite green sweater with its asymmetric hem, and in the bag beneath the chair she discovered fresh undies, socks and both her make-up and toiletries bags.

How on earth had her possessions arrived at Ruy's house? Had Cecile told Suzy's father where she was and had her father packed a bag for her and brought it over while she slept? Sudden guilt that she had still not phoned her father washed over her. But in truth, she had yet to work out how much she could risk telling the older man about the breakdown of her relationship with Percy.

She washed and dressed very quickly and didn't bother with any make-up, sensitive now to what Ruy might assume if she appeared to be gilding the lily for his benefit. After all, a man who could thank a woman for *not* inviting him into bed had shameless confidence and a daunting, meteoric awareness of the strength of his own attractiveness. Suzy planned to do nothing and say nothing that might encourage such arrogance. Hadn't she already done enough with that stupid kiss? Hopefully he would put that down to her disorientation after she had almost been frozen into a Popsicle.

As she moved towards the door, a knock sounded on it and she tugged it open, startled to find Ruy standing there holding a tray. 'What's this?' she muttered.

'It was supposed to be breakfast in bed, but I can see I left it too late,' Ruy fielded with amusement.

'Ruy,' Suzy admonished with a raised auburn brow. 'I've never had breakfast in bed in my life. I'm more likely to be serving it to other people than enjoying it myself.'

'That may be but there is always a first time,' Ruy retorted, refusing to be sidetracked and settling the tray down on the circular table by the window. 'Sit down, *eat...*'

'Gosh, you must keep your housekeeper busy,' Suzy remarked in wonderment at the beautifully set tray with its ornamental cloth and fresh orange juice, pastries, fruit and tea, all proffered in the finest china along with a seasonal lilac blossom in a tiny vase. 'This is beautiful. Make sure you thank her for me. She went to a lot of trouble.'

'I will,' Ruy promised, impressed by her thoughtfulness because so many of the women he knew took excellent service entirely for granted.

'When did Dad drop my clothes off? You should have wakened me,' Suzy scolded as she drank her orange juice, still pacing the room.

'He gave the bag to me last night. Mrs Liggett brought it up but found you asleep.'

Her smooth pale brow had furrowed. 'You saw my father last night? Oh, you went to the pub for a drink.'

'No, I went specifically to see him and we talked in private,' Ruy extended, lounging back against the bedroom door with folded arms and narrowed dark perceptive eyes locked to her restless movements. Sunlight burnishing her hair, she was full of energy but growing tension was threaded through that energy like iron bars strengthening concrete, he conceded, amused by that analogy but well aware of the questioning onslaught of her bright eyes and the volatile force of nature that powered her deceptively small and slender frame. He found it strange that her volatility, which had troubled him at the outset of their acquaintance, now only drew him in faster.

'Why would you go to see my father?' Suzy asked with a frown.

'To make life a little smoother for you,' Ruy countered lazily. 'When I see a problem, I tend to solve it. In fact, I excel at solving problems.'

Suzy tossed her head back in irritation. '*My* problems are not *your* problems!'

Unperturbed, Ruy spread the fingers of one lean hand and began marking off points. 'One… I detest abusers and I wanted you to feel free to report your ex to the police. Two… I knew that you wouldn't accept the money to pay off Brenton from me…you told me so. Three… I want to make it possible for you to act as my model without other concerns getting in the way. Four… I would also like you to accompany me to my brother's wedding. Five…if you think of this situation from a logical point of view, our mutual needs can dovetail perfectly.'

Suzy's chest heaved as she snatched in short breath after short breath in an effort to control her temper. She wanted to slap his point-scoring fingers off his hand. She wanted to deprive him utterly of the ability to stand there telling her without embarrassment that he had approached *her* father behind *her* back on her supposed behalf. 'I don't know what you've done... I'm not even sure I *want* to know!' she exclaimed. 'Did you tell Dad that Percy attacked me?'

'Yes, and while he was very angry he knows that you're not seriously hurt.'

'You have no right to interfere in my life!' Suzy hurled at him.

'The pub belongs to your father, *not* to you, and what arrangements he chooses to make with me are entirely his business,' Ruy spelt out, dropping her back down to earth again with a crash. 'As it happens, I've bought a share in the pub. I will be a silent partner, but it takes the pressure off your father. He will be able to repay Brenton without difficulty, although, as I told him, he could take him to court over the paperwork, which did not clearly specify the interest rate Brenton was charging. But your father prefers to let that go—he's not keen on the idea of calling in a solicitor.'

Suzy had gone white with mounting shock and dismay. 'You've bought a share in our pub?' she gasped in disbelief. 'But why the heck would you do that?'

'I live locally now, although I won't be resident here throughout the year. It's an investment. A pub is an asset in a village,' Ruy pronounced, as though he were not aware that the business was struggling. 'Now it will stay open and your father remains the landlord.'

'I just don't believe this!' Suzy confessed in seething frustration.

'I had to find some way around your reluctance to accept my financial help,' Ruy pointed out without shame.

'But don't you see that what you've done is *wrong*?' Suzy demanded angrily. 'That you've simply found another way of bribing me and getting me to do what you want? Evidently, you only bought into the pub to manipulate me!'

'Your father is happy, and you love your father. I don't see what the problem is or how it can be wrong when I have only good intentions,' Ruy declared, brilliant dark eyes challenging hers.

'I know you're not likely to beat me up, but you leave Percy standing in the ruthless stakes!' Suzy condemned.

'That is possible,' Ruy conceded without surprise or regret. 'I always play to win. When I want something, I do go all out to get it.'

'I'm a person, not a something!' Suzy hissed censoriously. 'I already agreed that I would try to model for you. At no cost! There was no need for you to go behind my back and invest in the pub!'

'Set aside my financial investment in your father's business,' Ruy advised. 'It is nothing to do with you, except insofar as it means that you can now stop worrying about your father's security.'

In a passion of confusion and incredulity, Suzy folded her arms and spun away from him. 'Nothing will convince me that you had a sincere interest in buying a share of the pub!' she shot at him.

Ruy shrugged a broad shoulder. 'I'm not trying to convince you. I don't have to justify what I've done, but I would make the point that your father is very happy with his side of the bargain and even more relieved to know that Percy is out of both your lives.'

Suzy's slender hands knotted into fists. 'Damn you!' she snapped at him, because every time she thought she had him on a weak spot he leapt away and put her there instead. 'You drive me insane!'

'And your passion lights me up,' Ruy confided in a raw undertone, needing to touch her almost as badly as he needed to paint her, flexing his long fingers and coiling them up again, rigid with the tension of unsated arousal.

Never before had he been with such an emotional woman. He had learned to repress his own emotions. He slept with women who had no drama to irritate him and he could not begin to explain or understand what it was about Suzy's volatility that made her so very desirable. That trait, that essential fire in her, *should* have been a turn-off and yet, it wasn't. She was not his type, categorically *not* his type, but when she went toe to toe with him, fists knotted, eyes shimmering in challenge like polished malachite, pink pouty lips parted to display little pearl-like teeth, it turned him on so hard and fast that the zip of his jeans bit a pattern into his throbbing flesh.

'Your control, your coldness, has the opposite effect on me,' Suzy confided tautly. 'It makes me want to shake you up.'

'Success…*major* success on that score,' Ruy purred with an emphasis that seemed to glide down her rigid spine like caressing fingers.

Suzy's knees wobbled a little. 'We really are oil and water,' she muttered uneasily.

'No, we're more like a conflagration,' Ruy husked, stalking closer, suddenly seeming to snatch all the oxygen out of the air she needed to breathe. 'And it's a fire I don't want to put out because, like any man, I *love* the burn, *querida*.'

'I'm shouting at you. You can't change the subject in the middle of an argument,' Suzy told him loftily.

'That's the look I want when you lift your

chin…just like that.' Ruy angled up her chin with a fingertip, let it slide back down the cord of her neck to her clavicle, where it lingered. 'And you look at me like you're a queen and I'm a filthy peasant. No woman has ever looked at me like that.'

'You have the most wildly extravagant imagination,' Suzy remarked unevenly, stepping back a few inches, the skin of her neck tingling, tenderly aware of that light touch, so very different from Percy's harsh, careless grip on her arm, her elbow or her shoulder. Her shoulders met with the wall. She had honestly believed that Percy didn't know his own strength. How naïve had she been in believing that that occasional roughness was simply masculine, careless and unintentional?

Her gaze locked to Ruy's lean dark features and something sweet and yet almost painful clenched low in her pelvis and for the first time she recognised what was happening to her body. She regretted that she had got halfway through her twenty-second year before experiencing normal sexual attraction. The race of her pulse, the hammer of her heart, the sudden tightening of her nipples as well as the dryness of her mouth held her fast because she had never felt anything that powerful before and she was remembering *that* kiss, that brief but glorious adrenalin rush.

Dark golden eyes welded to hers, Ruy stalked slowly closer and her heart raced so fast it felt as though it were thumping at the foot of her throat. He reached for her and if he hadn't reached for her she reckoned that she would have shamelessly grabbed him.

'You want this?' Ruy breathed in a driven undertone, easing her closer, one hand braced on her hip, the other braced against the wall behind her.

'I want...you,' she heard herself say and she didn't know where the words came from, only that it was a truth so new to her that she *had* to say it, *had* to share it.

'Gracias a Dios,' Ruy groaned above her head, crushing her mouth under his with an urgency that shook her to her very depths. His mouth contrived to communicate every-

thing she didn't have the words to express and the explosive effect of his hunger meeting hers set her on fire.

It took a while in that passionate exchange of kisses for Suzy to notice that he was extracting her from her sweater and for a split second she stilled, checking with herself that that was all right. And because it was Ruy, because she was so worked up that she was wound up tighter than a spring, it was fine. She was a big girl now, she reminded herself abstractedly, not a teenager keeping a handsy first boyfriend within acceptable limits. Yes, she could take her clothes off now, of course she could.

'Of course, you would have to have *the* boots on.' Ruy sighed, lifting her up into his arms and bringing her down onto the side of the bed, crouching down lithely at her feet to remove her boots. 'I love these boots. You're going to wear them in the studio for me when you pose—'

'Am I?' Amusement softened Suzy's gaze as she stared down at him, spearing her fingers into his black luxuriant hair, smooth-ing it back from his brow, admiring the dark slashing brows and the ridiculously long ebony lashes framing his gorgeous eyes. Ab-sently she wondered what she had thought about before she met him.

'In a wedding dress…but not the one you put on for *him*,' he asserted, tossing aside the boots and gently pushing her back to embark on the zip of her jeans.

'You have the most crazy imagination.' Suzy sighed.

'I'm not an imaginative man.'

'But you're an artist. You've got to be imaginative,' Suzy told him, sensing that for some reason he was in denial of that reality. 'I mean, imagining me posing in my boots and a wedding dress…how eccentric is th… that?' She stammered to a halt as, with one hard yank, he succeeded in tugging the jeans down her long slender legs.

'But that's not imagination, that's the reality of how I saw you in the woods,' Ruy argued, lifting her dangling legs up onto the divan and coming down beside her. 'We're talking too much… I don't talk in bed—'

'Tough,' Suzy whispered, touching a fingertip to his slightly reddened lips. 'Two people here, two votes, not just one…you just revel in being bossy, Ruy.'

He hauled off his sweater and leant over her, shimmering dark golden eyes alight as flames against his bronzed complexion, the corner of his mouth hinting at a smile. 'Maybe a little.'

'I should've run like hell when you told me about buying into the pub,' Suzy remarked with sudden anxiety. 'Maybe you're one of those controlling guys, who tries to own a woman.'

'I've never tried to own a woman in my life. And you see this is why you don't talk in bed—it gets too serious and now you're freaking yourself out and stressing again,' Ruy censured, dropping a kiss down on her parted lips, trailing his own slowly down her neck to her shoulder, lighting up a tingling trail of arousal through her trembling body.

'I'm still furious with you!' she protested, struggling to ground herself again and yet at the same time inwardly rejoicing at the concept of her own freedom from constraint, the precious ability to do as she liked for once.

All her life, after all, she had been the good dutiful daughter, instinctively tailoring herself to the role her father needed her to fill. She hadn't had the liberty to choose a career once she had grasped that her father couldn't afford to pay anyone else for the work she did. In the same way she hadn't experimented with any young men because, working at the pub, she couldn't risk acquiring a free and easy reputation, which would only encourage the often married men who tried to chat her up.

'Why would you be?' Ruy reasoned in what appeared to be genuine surprise as he stared down at her with smouldering dark golden eyes. 'I'm solving problems for you.'

'But I don't *need* you to solve my problems.'

'There's no shame in accepting help when it's available.' Ruy kissed a rousing trail across one delicate shoulder, lingering on her collarbone, making her shiver convulsively, heat curling at the secret heart of her. 'I'll be disappointed if you decide not to model for me or accompany me to Spain but if those are the choices you make, I will respect them,' he swore.

With those words, that assurance that she was still free to do as she wished, he broke the last chain of constraint holding her back. Bribery and blackmail only worked with the addition of pressure and he was removing the threat of that pressure. 'You promise?' she pressed tightly.

'I promise, *querida*,' Ruy husked, lean fingers spreading across her curvy derriere to angle her into collision with his erection. 'I can take no for an answer when to do otherwise would make a woman feel intimidated.'

Her heart raced as she felt his readiness. 'Take off your clothes,' she urged helplessly, impatient and greedy now that he had soothed her fears.

Ruy vaulted off the bed and stripped at

speed. Boots, sweater, jeans hit the floor in a messy heap, leaving him standing there before her for a split second, almost naked, and breathtaking in a way she had never known a man could be. He was very tall, very lean and all muscle from his sculpted torso and flat, corrugated stomach to his powerful arms and legs. Her attention lingered on the thrusting evidence of his arousal, clearly delineated by the boxers he sported, and her face burned, curiosity and anxiety melding as he strode into the bathroom and reappeared to toss a handful of condoms down beside the bed.

A handful? Surely he wasn't planning on them doing the deed more than once?

He released the catch on her bra, cupped a firm full mound and suckled a straining nipple and an arrow of damp heat raced through her and settled into a dulled throb between her thighs. Her spine arched as she surged up to him, alight as a crackling fire craving oxygen. His mouth crashed down on hers again and the heat inside her surged even higher. Her hands danced over every part of him she could reach, toying with his hair, caressing his wide smooth shoulders, skating down the long line of his flexing back, fingers curling as he addressed his attention to her other breast and tugged on the sensitive tip until she moaned low in her throat.

An impatience more powerful than anything she had ever felt assailed her. Hunger clawed at her, a wanting, a need she had never before experienced. He took her mouth again, urgently tasting her, and every delve of his tongue made her temperature rocket.

He lifted his dark head, struggling to catch his breath. 'Slow down,' he urged. 'We're not in a hurry.'

Her eyes closed tight against the compelling contours of his beautiful face, defiance racing through her trembling frame because she didn't like to be controlled and just then, as the giver of pleasure, he was controlling her. He might not be in a hurry, but she *was*. She ran a hand down over his flat stomach and stroked him, surprised by how smooth and yet hard, like steel wrapped in velvet, he was, delighted when he shuddered against her and groaned out loud, as responsive to her as she was to him and she liked that, really *liked* that feeling of power. She pressed him back against the pillows.

A glint lighting his dark golden gaze, Ruy used his hands to roll her over instead. 'This that two-vote equality thing you mentioned earlier?' he teased huskily, stretching a hand down to whisk off her panties before reaching for protection.

'Maybe...' Arms wrapping round him, Suzy pulled him down to her again, nibbling at his lower lip before passionately kissing him, unable to sate her longing for his mouth on hers again.

Ruy traced a finger over her swollen wet centre and a whimper of sound was torn from her as she lifted up to him by instinct, desperate to ease the drumbeat of need driving her, barely recognising herself when she was lost in that fierce craving. He slid between her trembling thighs and entered her in a powerful surge, and she jerked at the burn of his entrance into her untried body. It hurt and she gritted her teeth, shocked because she hadn't expected pain. She closed her eyes tight and endured until the burn lessened, faded, turned into something else, a something that soothed and aroused and entrapped her afresh.

A ripple of excitement built in her pelvis and the promise of pleasure was so strong it held her spellbound. He felt extraordinary. Waves of heat and sensation shimmered through her sensitised body, exquisite sensation tugging at her with every thrust of his lean, powerful length. He ground down on her and went deeper and her world just exploded round her in a white-hot electrifying shower of response that lit her up inside and out. She tumbled back against the pillows, shattered by that climax, fascinated by an experience that had been so much more powerful than she had ever dreamt it could be.

Ruy pulled back from her and immediately saw the blood on her thighs and on him and he remembered the way she had hidden her face, the incredible tightness of her, and suddenly he registered that he had been a complete idiot and he was furious. Nobody was less able to cope with the suspicion that he had slept with a virgin than Ruy. Indeed, he had gone through a phase after his nightmare with Liliana of checking beforehand that no woman he slept with was an innocent. As a rule, though, the risk wasn't great because Ruy rarely took younger women to bed.

'How old are you?' he suddenly demanded of Suzy.

Her smooth brow furrowing at the rawness of that enquiry, Suzy sat up. 'Twenty-one… why?'

Dark golden eyes as hard and unyielding as the stone in his bathroom, Ruy surveyed her grimly and sprang off the bed. 'You were a virgin. I had no idea and I wouldn't have touched you had you warned me.'

'*Warned* you?' she repeated in shaken objection to his attitude. 'Why would I have warned you?'

'Because I didn't sign up for this scenario,'

Ruy lanced back chillingly. 'I don't sleep with virgins...*ever*! I don't want you attaching expectations to what just happened between us because sex means virtually nothing to me. I'm not about to fall madly in love with you and suggest that we have a serious relationship either... I don't work that way. I'm sorry.'

A shuddering wave of humiliation engulfed Suzy as she stared back at him in shock. Unapologetic eyes challenged hers before he swung away to stride into the bathroom and the door slammed shut.

CHAPTER FIVE

SUZY STAYED STILL for only a few moments and then she leapt off the bed and ran around scooping up her clothes, clambering back into them as fast as she could. At the same time, a phone started buzzing somewhere, a phone she suspected to be in Ruy's discarded jeans. Ignoring it, she sped downstairs, not even sure where she was going. She felt hurt, humiliated, utterly and cruelly exposed after his cutting words in the aftermath of their intimacy. She had got into bed with the wrong guy, totally the wrong guy.

In the spacious lounge area, she looked around in search of the studio he had mentioned or at least the possibility of another bathroom facility because she knew she had to wash the memory of him off her skin. She peered into an empty kitchen, a cloakroom and then a big airy room with full-height windows that overlooked the dense woods. It contained both an easel, a stack of canvases and a bed. One of the doors off it led into a bathroom and with a sigh of relief she began to undress again.

She had gone to bed with a man she barely knew, and she cursed her impulsive nature for that blunder. She had leapt in where angels feared to tread. All the worst mistakes she had ever made could be laid at the door of that flaw in her character. Well, lesson learned, she told herself urgently, frantically striving to fill the deep well of pain inside her with more positive feelings. Her body ached, reminding her of what she wanted to most forget.

How on earth had she put herself in a position where Ruy Rivera could reject her as if she had chased after him begging for his attention? Was he so arrogant, so vain that he assumed every woman would try to entrap him if she got the chance? What else was she to think after that speech he had made?

Plenty more fish in the sea, one of her friends at school used to quip when some boy let her down, but just then Suzy didn't believe she would ever dare to look at a man again with covetous eyes.

On the floor above, Ruy almost punched the wall of his shower, drawing his clenched fist back with a curse at the last possible moment. What the hell had come over him when he verbally attacked Suzy like that? But he *knew*, didn't he? He knew all too well where that attack of paranoia had come from. His brain had succumbed to a flashback of Liliana and the catastrophic trail of events that she had initiated in his life. Cold revulsion and disquiet had drenched Ruy like an acid bath and he had lashed out accordingly at an innocent. He gritted his teeth. Ruy had never liked being in the wrong and even less did he like the prospect of apologising.

A virgin though, he hadn't been prepared for that possibility at all. Why not though? She was still very young, *too* young for him, he censured himself. He had given in to lust like a sex-starved teenager with no thought of the consequences. As a result, he had destroyed any trust Suzy might have had in him and any hope of her being willing to do anything for him. He towelled himself off grimly and stooped to snatch up his phone when he heard it buzzing.

Damp and breathless from her haste, Suzy emerged back into the lounge, having decided what she would do next. She would nip back upstairs, collect her stuff and then go home to her father. She would have to walk back by the road, which would take ages, but she didn't feel as though she had a choice. She reckoned she would sooner walk over hot coals than spend another hour under Ruy Rivera's roof.

Someone thumped loudly on the front door knocker. Suzy frowned, knowing the housekeeper wasn't around and that Ruy was probably still in the shower. After a moment of hesitation, she opened the front door and took a dumbfounded step back as Percy confronted her with knotted fists and an enraged red face.

'You slut!' he launched at her accusingly. 'So, the rumours were true!'

'Leave me alone!' Suzy exclaimed as he extended his thick arms to grab at her and she snaked backwards into the safety of the house.

As Percy lurched past the door she attempted to slam shut in his face, two things happened. She saw several men racing across the driveway towards them and heard someone coming down the stairs to her rear.

With an explosive Spanish curse, Ruy thrust Suzy to safety behind him and as Percy ploughed forward Ruy punched him hard. Percy went down like rock and, venting a hissed imprecation, Ruy grabbed him by the scruff of the neck and dragged him out of the house. Suzy was frozen to the spot, shocked by the speed of Ruy's reactions. She watched as four men rushed up the steps, frantically apologising to Ruy in Spanish while grabbing hold of Percy to haul him away.

'Who the heck are they?' Suzy whispered shakily.

'Staff,' Ruy breathed curtly. 'Did he hurt you?'

'No...you got here just in time.'

'My staff let him onto the grounds because they knew you were staying here and they assumed that he was your father,' Ruy explained with a shake of his head, damp black hair tousled above dark deep-set eyes that shone gold with strong emotion. 'Well, they won't make that mistake again and we will ensure that Brenton stays away.'

'Don't know how we're going to do that... Percy likes to have his say,' Suzy muttered as Ruy paced away from her, punching a number on his phone and speaking rapidly.

'Legal counsel will meet us at the police station...'

Suzy dealt him a dazed look, still reeling from Percy's sudden appearance and the shockingly efficient violence of Ruy's response. She watched as the men Ruy had labelled staff levered Percy back into his car and stood back waiting for him to drive away. 'Why would we need legal counsel?'

And *why*, in concert with Ruy, was she suddenly employing that royal 'we' as if Ruy were as ensnared in the ongoing problem of Percy as she was?

'You have to apply for a non-molestation order to keep Brenton at a distance but first you must report the original assault to the police,' Ruy told her firmly. 'You really can't afford to wait to do that now.'

'No,' Suzy conceded with a shudder, her ex's second attempt to assault her having shaken her up badly and made her appreciate that she did need the law to protect her.

'It'll take an hour for the solicitor I've instructed to arrive.'

'I don't know why you would be instructing a solicitor to help me,' Suzy told him flatly, shooting him a bemused glance. 'You know your moods change like the wind, Ruy. One minute you're Mr Nice guy, the *next*—'

Watching her warily, Ruy expelled his

breath in a hiss. 'Will you allow me to apologise and explain?'

Suzy stiffened and flushed; her expressive
eyes carefully veiled. 'You don't need to explain anything to me.'

'I apologise for what I said upstairs,' Ruy
murmured in a driven undertone, thoroughly
surprising her with that candid opening.

'Unfortunately,' he continued flatly, 'after
an experience I had with a woman eight years
ago, I'm a little paranoid about having sex
with a virgin.'

'A *little*?' Suzy stressed. 'Anyone could
have been forgiven for thinking I was ready
to set a wedding date!'

But his frankness and the speed of his apol-
ogy had already struck a reassuring note
with Suzy. Clearly, Ruy had faults and bag-
gage just as she did, a little voice piped up
inside her head, and he was strong enough
to admit those facts. He had helped her, had
dealt with Percy and was still fully commit-
ted to ensuring that she stayed safe. Yes, Ruy
had also said stuff he shouldn't have said and

made assumptions that he was not entitled to make, but if he was willing to explain she decided she would listen even if it was only out of curiosity. Stiff with nervous tension, she dropped down on the edge of a sofa and studied him with caution.

Ruy was currently engaged in buttoning the shirt he had put on with his jeans. He had been bare-chested when he repelled Percy, the shirt fluttering loose. He was now covering that broad slice of bronzed muscular torso. As a little spark of heat awakened low in her belly, she turned pink and swiftly averted her attention from him. 'Eight years ago, you must have been quite young,' she remarked uncomfortably.

'I was twenty-two,' Ruy admitted flatly. 'I took a woman home from a club one evening. She was a virgin and afterwards she spooked me by announcing that she had always known that we would make a wonderful couple. I had never met her before and, at that age, I was more into one-night stands than anything else. Regrettably, she decided that that one night constituted a relationship and she turned into a stalker, who caused me a lot of trouble and unhappiness.'

'Oh, my goodness,' Suzy groaned in surprise and sympathy at his explanation.

'So perhaps you can now understand why I forgot my manners for a moment with you and dived straight into mistrust. What happened with that woman did a lot of damage to my life. Since then I have generally been much more careful about the women I take as lovers and they have, until now, always been more mature and experienced.'

'I think the lady's problems had very little to do with her lack of sexual experience.'

'You're right, but that lack was the only thing that made her different from her predecessors. I'm afraid discovering your innocence unleashed my worst memories.'

'I can understand that...now that I know about your past,' Suzy extended, wanting to ask him more about his stalking experience, but, sensing that he had shared as much as he felt comfortable sharing with her, she reluctantly suppressed her curiosity.

'Now go upstairs and put your boots on. We're going to the police station,' Ruy informed her.

'Right now?' she gasped.

'No better time.'

Apprehensive at the prospect of reporting Percy to the police, Suzy got to her feet, ruefully amused that she had left her boots upstairs and had been running around in her socks without realising it. Putting on her boots, she came down again clutching her bag and tossing it into the car that Ruy stood beside.

'You'll feel relieved when it's done,' he assured her confidently.

Some time later Suzy emerged from the police station, answering the urbane solicitor, Ellis Johnson's query about the nearest good hotel. The imaginary weight she had felt on her chest had lifted and, for the first time in several days, she felt a little more like herself again. Ruy planted a light hand to her slender spine to urge her back into his vehicle while

Ellis headed for his own car. She knew that she had to go back home with Ruy to fill out the paperwork for the non-molestation order with Ellis. The recollection of Percy forcing his way into Ruy's house still had the power to make her blood run cold. She registered that it would take time for her to stop feeling jumpy and feel safe again.

'Will you consider signing a non-disclosure agreement with Ellis at the same time?' Ruy enquired without warning. 'With a view to modelling for me? I know you're probably not in the right mood to contemplate anything extra and understandably you may feel that you can't trust me now.'

Without even thinking about it, Suzy lifted her hand to rest it soothingly down on a long powerful thigh in disagreement. 'No. I don't feel that way. You were very honest with me and I appreciate that but, after all the strife and hassle I've brought into your life, I can't believe that you *still* want to paint me.'

'That hasn't changed.'

'OK, then,' Suzy breathed. 'But I'm not

sure about going to Spain yet…although the thought of the locals piling into the pub just to stare at me and speculate about what happened with Percy makes me cringe.'

'Someone somewhere will talk. They won't have to speculate for long,' Ruy forecast. 'As to Spain, I haven't been very professional in my approach, but I can assure you that I'm not about to put pressure on you to continue our liaison.'

'Not sure I can make the same promise,' Suzy confided without thinking through what she was admitting, because she was thinking that that word, 'liaison', had a certain sensual buzz on his lips and lent their brief encounter a distinct sophistication.

Ruy flashed her a startled glance from glittering dark golden eyes and then threw back his handsome head and laughed out loud with appreciation. 'Suzy…where have you been all my life?'

'I shouldn't have said that,' Suzy muttered, her face burning, only then lifting her hand off his thigh where it had lingered. Somewhere deep down inside her she felt extraordinarily comfortable and relaxed with Ruy and she was mortified, particularly after he had declared that sex meant nothing to him.

And she completely understood that attitude if he'd had the amount of practice she suspected. Sex was neither new nor particularly tempting for him. It was an activity he had taken for granted and freely enjoyed, most probably with women who were a great deal more beautiful and sensually talented than she was. For her their encounter had been a major event but it was highly unlikely that it had been equally exciting for him. Why else would he be telling her that he would be putting no further pressure on her to repeat the experience? And why had she said what she had? She had been joking, trying to lighten her embarrassment at the topic being discussed, but that particular joke had backfired on her. Surely, he wouldn't think that she had meant that seriously?

Back at the house Ellis Johnson explained the non-disclosure agreement to her in fine detail. Signing the document would prevent her from ever speaking or writing about anything relating to Ruy, or indeed posting photos of him or his work, but it didn't strike her as an onerous promise to make because she had never been much given to gossip or social media. In any case she was fairly certain that, once Ruy had painted her, he would have no further interest in her and, by the sound of it, he spent most of his time in Spain. He would melt back out of her life as quickly as he had entered it, she reasoned ruefully, wondering why that should be a deflating thought. Perhaps prior to meeting Ruy, and even prior to Percy, she had allowed her life to become too boring and predictable.

'If I could just get my bag out of your car I can go home now,' she told Ruy as Ellis stood up to leave.

'You have to stay for lunch. You still haven't eaten…and your father was planning to call in here to see you this afternoon,' Ruy imparted while Ellis stared at her and then at Ruy as though he was fascinated by the exchange.

'Dad's coming *here*?' Suzy said in surprise.

'When you go through a traumatic event you have to sit down and catch your breath after it,' Ruy informed her. 'Now it's time to rest and *relax*...'

Her green eyes widened. 'Is it professional for you to still be telling me what to do?' she enquired.

Ruy shrugged, impervious to insult. 'I have more common sense than you do, *querida*.'

'Says the man who thinks he knows everything. Why am I not surprised?' Suzy tossed back, flushing when she noticed Ellis still staring as he departed.

'If you do decide to come to Spain to accompany me to my brother's wedding, I will need to know everything about you,' Ruy admitted over lunch. 'Your birthday, likes and dislikes, everything a fiancé would be expected to know.'

'If I decide to go, I'll draw up a cheat sheet for you and you would need to do the same for me,' she pointed out. 'I'm good at memorising stuff.'

'Why did you choose to stay in the village

at the pub instead of moving somewhere that would have offered you more options?'

'Dad needed me. Sometimes you have to do things you don't want to do. My life's always been like that. I've learned to deal.'

'Your father adores you,' Ruy incised. 'He would hate to know how you really feel.'

'It's always been Dad and I against the world…it's all I know. He has often suggested that I go off travelling or try working somewhere else, but I persuaded him that I was a home bird. I don't want him to feel guilty about it. How much did you tell him about Percy?'

'That's your department. I glossed over the nastier elements, played ignorant. I don't think your father needs to know that Brenton was blackmailing you right under his nose, but I do think he suspects that you were only marrying the man to help him.'

Suzy gave him a grateful look. 'Thanks. That was tactful.'

Her father wrapped her into a tight hug as soon as he arrived and studied her with tears shining in his searching gaze. Ruy went into his studio to leave them in peace to talk.

'I can come home now,' Suzy told the older man.

Roger Madderton frowned. 'I thought you were staying on here, because people are asking a lot of nosy questions and—'

'Don't you need help at the pub?'

'I'm managing fine.' He reminded her that he had hired Flora to cover for her. 'If you'd married Percy, you'd have been gone for good and as it is now, with that loan off my back, I can afford to pay for any help I need.'

Her father was also keen to share exciting news for the future with her. A stately home a few miles away was opening up to the public for the first time and he reckoned that the pub would gain custom from tourists. 'Ruy knew about it, of course. He's very much on the ball when it comes to business,' he opined with a slow admiring shake of his head. 'Taking yourself off to Spain with him for a week is a brilliant idea. You deserve a break after what Percy has put you through.'

'Ruy told you about Spain?' Suzy gasped in surprise.

'Getting away is exactly what you need and if he wants to paint you sitting under an orange tree or some such weird arty thing, let him do it…no skin off your nose!' The older man chuckled, his amusement at such an ambition unconcealed.

Registering that her father had no knowledge of the pretend fiancée role that Ruy wanted her to accept, Suzy smiled without committing herself. It hurt a little that her father wasn't gasping to bring her home, but then that was partly because he knew how much she would cringe at receiving pitying looks and awkward questions from their customers. What astonished her, however, was his faith in Ruy.

'You like him…why?' she asked baldly as the older man was leaving.

'He stepped up for you when you needed it—it wasn't his problem but that didn't matter to him. He did what was right. I respect that in a man,' Roger Madderton replied, and then turned to go back to his car.

Suzy knocked on the studio door, opening it when Ruy called out.

'How did you make my father your biggest fan?' she asked softly.

Tossing aside his sketchbook, Ruy lifted a broad shoulder in a fluid shrug of dismissal. He knew that the truth would be tasteless. Her father had been worn down with worry about the pub and losing that fear had given him a new lease of life. 'Although he's furious that you were hurt, he's very relieved that you're not marrying Brenton.'

'He's not the only one of us relieved,' Suzy conceded, spiralling curls of copper falling across her pale cheek, her green eyes reflective, her skin translucent in the stark daylight, her lips a plump and rosy contrast.

Tensing, Ruy glanced away, suppressing his response to her because it was destroying his concentration. No model had ever had that effect on him before. But then, until

Suzy, his relationship with his models had been strictly business and devoid of any sexual element. Why was it different with her? Why couldn't he retain his detachment with her? He had assumed that sex would remove much of her mysterious allure, although that was not why he had ended up in bed with her.

No, he had ended up in bed with her because hunger had overpowered restraint and passion had silenced every logical reservation. That had never happened to Ruy before and such a weakness, such an inability to withstand temptation, disturbed the legendary even temperament that he cherished. It was even more daunting that in spite of acknowledging the folly of a sexual connection with his model he still only had to look at Suzy to want her afresh. And *this* was the woman he was choosing to take home with him? The very first woman who would learn that Ruy Valiente was also V, the famous portrait painter, who scrupulously conserved his anonymity? He crushed the thought in favour of focussing on what was most important to him.

'Will you come to Spain with me?' Ruy pressed softly.

Suzy wondered if Ruy had always had that innate ESP that told him the optimum moment to pose a thorny question. She studied him, her gaze lingering on the black spiky lashes framing his stunning eyes, the angle of a hard cheekbone in sunlight, the sensual curve of his moulded lips. He was beautiful but it was the sheer driving force of will behind that façade that worried her the most. He hadn't been joking when he said that when he wanted something he went all out to get it. He never, it seemed, forgot his objective for an instant. It was a decidedly unnerving trait, but her father's opinion of him had eased her misgivings and even made her feel a little foolish for backing nervously away from Ruy and his proposition.

'Yes, I'll accompany you,' she stated. 'I'll start my list of cheat-sheet questions today.'

'You'll also be trying on wedding gowns for me this afternoon.'

'I beg your pardon?' Suzy believed that she had misheard him.

'I want to paint you in a wedding dress but *not* the same one I found you in. I've ordered a selection to be brought here this afternoon and I'll choose the most suitable. Then you can go for a walk in the woods or something and dirty it up…add a strategic rip or two…' Ruy shifted a careless hand that implied such behaviour was so normal as not to require further explanation.

'You'll have to cut the dress if you want rips,' Suzy told him, striving not to sound as though she considered the concept to be strange. 'I tore my dress climbing the tree and jumping out of it and I'm not doing that again.'

'You can pose for the rough drawings here, but I plan to set the background in Spain. There's an orange grove at my home there.'

'You live on a fruit farm?' she asked with interest.

'There are orange orchards nearby,' Ruy parried, knowing he ought to tell her the truth, but holding out for as long as he could because he enjoyed her resolutely unimpressed attitude to him and he was afraid that unveiling the reality of his astronomic wealth would fatally change that.

And he preferred her as she was: an ordinary girl from an ordinary working background. Her breezy irreverence stemmed from that solid base. She had strong values. She respected hard work and was entirely free of snobbery. He had observed her in the pub and interacting with his nieces, learning that she was considerate towards the elderly and that she loved children, who loved her back because she was one of those adults who had never quite buried their inner child. Right now, she was relaxed with him, which was exactly how he needed her to be before he could paint her. How much would her outlook shift once she knew the truth about him?

'The stylist who is bringing the gowns will also be taking your measurements for the clothes you'll need to have for Spain,' Ruy volunteered casually.

'I don't need any new clothes for Spain. I have all the stuff I got for the honeymoon I was supposed to be having in Barbados,' Suzy pointed out.

'I doubt if there will be an outfit suitable for a high-society wedding. It won't be similar to a beach holiday where you throw on anything that's comfortable,' Ruy murmured drily.

'You can dress me however you like for painting...that's what artists do, isn't it?' Suzy asked uncertainly and then her triangular face tightened, her chin lifting, her bright eyes glinting back at him. 'But you don't get to tell me what to wear any other time or in any other place.'

'The clothes are merely props for the role you'll be carrying out for my benefit and I wouldn't be engaged to a woman who was poorly dressed.'

'My goodness, what a superficial person you are!' Suzy scoffed in exasperation. 'I said no, Ruy. Accept a refusal with grace.'

'Be realistic, Suzy,' Ruy breathed coolly. 'If this is about me buying you clothes, dump them when we part, but don't make this venture of ours more difficult than it needs to be!'

Suzy spun away from him, feeling rather as if she were trying to face down an invasion force. Given the smallest chance, Ruy would encroach a little way over the line, but if his initial incursion was successful, he would then flood in and take over at ridiculous speed and it infuriated her. She knew very well that nothing in her wardrobe would pass muster at an upmarket wedding. Ruy had been correct when he surmised that most of the stuff she had could be categorised as casual, rather than elegant or expensive. But he set her back up every time he came over all macho and bossy. Six months of having to dance to Percy's tune had made her touchy on that score.

Even so, Ruy had done her a huge favour when he'd helped her deal with Percy, she reminded herself, and now it was payback time. She whirled back to him, eyes defiant. 'You're making me feel like I'm the unreasonable one!' she condemned.

'It's a week of dressing up and acting attached to me...no big deal!' Ruy shot back at her.

Suzy settled her keen gaze on him. 'Ruy? Learn to quit when you're ahead. This is not the time to lay down the law and score points. I don't work for you. I'm not going to salute you and say, thank you, sir, what would you like me to do next?'

Ruy levered fluidly upright, long lean limbs effortlessly graceful, the power in his smouldering dark golden gaze illuminating his lean, devastatingly handsome features. 'No, you definitely don't want to ask me *that* question because you might not like my answer,' he breathed thickly.

Sixth sense prompted Suzy to back away until her shoulder blades met the window behind her. Sometimes when Ruy looked at her a certain way it felt like straying perilously close to a roaring blaze.

'On the other hand, you might like it too much,' Ruy completed huskily, gazing down at her with extraordinarily compelling golden eyes. 'And so might I.'

He traced her full lower lip with his finger-tip and her stomach turned over and her head swam and her knees felt weak, because he was close enough for her to smell the rawly familiar cologne-tinged scent of him. She teetered forward a few inches, *closer*. It was dangerous and she knew it was, knew that they were both attempting to respect boundaries and that, maddeningly, it was the most terrible struggle to do so.

'Kiss me,' he husked, his breath fanning her cheek, making her shiver with awareness.

And she stretched up and he stretched down and their lips collided, hers brushing back and forth with a tantalising lightness of touch, his hotter, harder, claiming her mouth with a fierce, impatient hunger that sent a shower of sparks licking up through her entire body. She had never wanted anything so much as she wanted that kiss to continue, but she also remembered the sensible limits she had promised herself that she would respect. She twisted her head away and sidestepped him, snatching in oxygen as though she had been drowning, denying the sensations rippling through her body in a seductive tide of response. The pulsing ache between her thighs hurt.

'I choose any clothes and I leave them behind when I'm done,' Suzy specified tightly, mentally washing away what had just happened between them, ignoring it as best she could.

Ruy clenched his teeth hard, rejection not being a reaction he had much experience with. It galled him that she had backed away first and that it had been the rational thing to do. Sex would muddy the waters of what was essentially a business arrangement, although it wasn't business when he wasn't paying her a fee, was it? And business didn't make him as hard as a rock with frustration either, he reasoned grimly.

'*And* we try to keep our connection friendly and…er…distant,' Suzy suggested shakily.

'Choose your battles with care, *querida*,' Ruy murmured sibilantly. 'I suspect we're both bad losers.'

CHAPTER SIX

'*SERIOUSLY?*' SUZY WHISPERED helplessly in Ruy's ear when he picked the wedding gown with the feathers. 'I'll roast alive wearing that in Spain.'

He spoke to the stylist about alterations with all the panache of one who knew what he was talking about, but his belief that the internal structure of the dress could essentially be ripped out to make it lighter simply exposed his ignorance. Suzy suppressed a chuckle, marvelling at his obstinacy and amazed by the dress he had picked while he continued to discuss options, expense clearly no drawback as it was agreed that the dress would literally be remade for the occasion. She had been expecting him to choose something severe and elegant, not extravagant and frothy and trailing white feathers like the ghost of Christmas past.

'Mr Rivera knows what he likes,' the stylist remarked when Ruy had left them alone and Suzy was able to get down to describing her requirements, which consisted of a single smart gown and accessories that would hopefully pass muster at his brother's wedding. But her taste in fashion was more quirky than conventional and it took time to identify a suitable dress for the wedding and the perfect shoes to wear with it.

The next morning she had to attend a court hearing in town for the non-molestation order Ellis had lodged on her behalf. Percy wasn't in attendance and the magistrate granted it. Ruy had accompanied her and she felt enormously grateful for his support and relieved when it was over. Afterwards, Ruy asked her to pose for him in the studio, wearing her jeans and sweater. She would have preferred to put some make-up on first, but he insisted that he didn't want her 'all painted up', as he called it. Sadly, that was only the start of their differences that afternoon. Ruy sketched while telling her how to pose in innumerable different positions. Every time she moved an inch or so out of a pose to ease a tight muscle, he growled in complaint and she shot comments back at him, telling him he needed to be more adaptable, more tolerant if he expected her to relax. Ruy liked his models quiet and biddable but as Suzy performed a handstand and then segued down into the splits with the easy flexibility of a dancer, he was too entertained by her joie de vivre to be exasperated.

Over dinner, she asked when they would be going to Spain.

'The day after tomorrow,' Ruy imparted.

'But the clothes won't have arrived by then.'

'They will. I made it clear that a longer wait wasn't an option,' Ruy extended calmly.

Suzy studied him in dismay. 'Ruy…someone could be up all night stitching that feather dress to meet a deadline like that!'

'I would expect that they will be handsomely remunerated if they are. I pay over the odds for good service,' he parried.

'Employees don't get those kinds of choices and I would assume that the boss usually keeps the profits.'

'That's the world we live in. Not my personal responsibility,' Ruy returned, impervious to the hint that he should be ashamed of his willingness to use money to ensure that he received exactly what he wanted when he wanted it, no matter how inconvenient and unreasonable his requests were. 'A jeweller will be calling here this evening for you to choose a ring for our supposed engagement, and at some stage you will have to go home to pick up whatever else you require for Spain.'

'You organise everything right down to the last tiny detail.' Suzy sighed. 'It doesn't leave much room for manoeuvre or going with the flow.'

'I wasn't raised to go with the flow,' Ruy murmured drily. 'I was brought up to respect rules and meet every demand that was made on me. It turned me into a high achiever. It's true that I don't turn handstands in the middle of a work session, but I value the discipline I learned.'

In receipt of that crack, Suzy felt the hot colour of embarrassment flood her cheeks. 'Sorry about that.'

'No, it was refreshing. One minute you were in place and the next you were upside down on the other side of the room,' Ruy pointed out with amusement. 'I won't get bored with you in the studio.'

Dinner was followed by the arrival of the jeweller complete with a security guard. Trays of rings were set out on the coffee table and Ruy closed a hand over hers and tugged her down beside him. 'Choose,' he urged calmly.

All Suzy could see was a crazy bank of glittering jewels. 'No, you choose.'

'Suzy,' Ruy murmured with the faintest emphasis.

The heat of a long thigh was against hers, warming her entire body and tugging at that insistent ache that stirred in her pelvis whenever she got too close to Ruy. It made her want to melt into him, over him, any way she could, but she resisted the urge to leap away, reminding herself that this was supposed to be a joyful occasion for a couple and that in a sense she was on stage and expected to act her part. She reached for a solitaire ring in the very centre.

'A most discerning choice,' the jeweller told her, practically purring at that selection, which implied to her that it was a very, *very* costly ring. 'The rarest of diamonds, a beautiful blue.'

'Perfect,' Ruy said, reaching for her trembling hand to thread it onto her finger, where it proved to be a little loose.

'Are you sure you like it?' Suzy prompted with anxious eyes.

'It's yours.'

Her finger was measured. The ring, she was assured, would be with them the next day. The jeweller and his guard departed.

'The ring will be yours to keep,' Ruy informed her.

Suzy froze in astonishment in receipt of

that assurance, angry resentment flaring inside her. 'No, you are doing it again—stop trying to buy me, bribe me, whatever you want to call it! I don't want that! I don't want you believing that you're paying me for any of this, but you don't listen, do you? Look, I have to collect my cases at home. I'll call Dad to pick me up and I'll go now, spend the night there,' she completed doggedly.

Ruy stilled in front of her, so tall, so dark, so devastatingly handsome, her senses hummed that close to him. *'Stay...'*

And it disturbed her that she *knew* he didn't want her to leave and that on some very basic level she was equally reluctant to move any great distance from him. Feeling that way was foolish and would hurt her, she told herself firmly. Was she planning to turn into some sort of clingy woman? That wasn't her, would *never* be her. She was sailing too close to the wind, risking her emotions for a guy who had no serious intentions whatsoever towards her. She was forgettable, *disposable* as far as Ruy was concerned. He had not once referred to their fleeting encounter beyond quickly assuring her that he did not expect her to continue that intimacy. How often did a guy turn his back on the chance of sex?

A guy that wasn't that keen, her brain told her bluntly, but then why was he so reluctant to let her leave his house? It was simple: Ruy wanted her to be on the spot and immediately available when the desire to sketch assailed him. Convenience meant everything to Ruy, who seemed to have a terminal objection to having to wait for anything.

'I'll run you back home,' Ruy volunteered when she said nothing.

Suzy breathed in deep and slow to ease her constricted lungs, knowing that she needed a little space to figure out why she felt so tied to Ruy. Because he had been around to save her when she was terrified? Because he had advised and supported her and made her feel safe? Was her brain, were her very emotions, really that basic? Or was she catching feelings for a man who would never catch them back?

* * *

She sat up late with her father and then went through her cases, discarding anything that seemed superfluous. Her father took her back to Ruy's the next morning and by then the wedding dress and her outfits had arrived and she went straight upstairs to try everything on. She walked downstairs in the feathered dress and Ruy sprang off the sofa where he was using a laptop and stared at her. In the gown, her fiery curls tumbling round her shoulders, she was a vision, a distinctly beautiful vision, not at all what he had originally planned.

'Do you still want me to dirty it up a bit?' Suzy enquired doubtfully.

'No, that idea won't work with that gown,' Ruy conceded. 'You could end up looking like a bedraggled bird after a rainstorm.'

Suzy giggled. 'That's what I thought.'

'I'll come up with something else.'

'From that non-existent fertile imagination of yours,' Suzy teased absently.

Ruy merely quirked a brow. He would still

paint her in the gown, but he would also paint her in her own clothes, immortalising those lovely delicate features of hers, the glow of her translucent skin and the grace of her. 'Let's do some work now,' he suggested with renewed enthusiasm.

The following day, Suzy rose early. She put on capri pants and a silky tee teamed with a short boxy jacket, aimed at giving her a more finished look. Her very high-heeled red sandals necessitated a slow descent of the stairs. She was surprised to see Ruy already downstairs, sheathed in a dark business suit that just screamed personal tailoring and expense. It fit him like a glove, accentuating his broad shoulders, narrow waist and long powerful legs.

'You're very formal,' she remarked, sitting down for breakfast.

'I like the pompoms on the shoes,' Ruy replied, evading that comment as he passed her a ring box. 'Very different.'

Suzy opened the box, removed the ring

and slid it onto her finger without ceremony before eating with appetite. She had only been abroad once and that had been a trip to Greece with a school friend's family the summer that she was sixteen. She was excited about visiting Spain, her late mother's birth place, but striving to act mature and hide the fact. When her cases had been carted away and she walked out of the house to see a limousine awaiting them, she was startled.

'Is this what you call travelling in style?'

'Something like that.'

'Which airport are we heading for?'

'I use a private airfield nearby. It's not far and it'll speed up our journey.'

A private airfield? How did that work? Reluctant to betray her ignorance, Suzy said nothing while wondering if he knew someone who had offered them flights on his plane.

They drew up at the office at the airfield. Ruy requested her passport and it was handed out of the limo to the man who emerged from the office. Suzy idly appraised the sleek white jet parked on the runway nearby. It bore a V logo and the Spanish flag on its tail.

'Time for us to board,' Ruy advised as the passenger door was opened by the driver.

The pilot and two stewardesses greeted them at the foot of the steps. There was a lot of what Suzy regarded as bowing and scraping and the ladies were very flirty with Ruy. Suzy frowned as she mounted the steps and moved into what struck her as the very last word in opulent cabin interiors. There were reclining seats, coffee tables, polished wood, pale leather surfaces, and through the arch at the foot she could see an actual conference table surrounded by chairs. She stepped back as the four men she had seen at Ruy's secluded home passed by them and headed towards the back of the plane, where they disappeared from view.

'Make yourself comfortable,' Ruy advised.

'A private jet?' Suzy queried, settling stiffly down into a reclining seat but keeping it upright, quite unable to relax in so sumptuous a setting.

Ruy vented a rueful laugh, raw charisma in the lazy half-smile he angled in her direction. 'I suppose it's time to come clean.'

'I think it is,' Suzy agreed with a dangerous glint in her clear green eyes. 'You have access to a private jet or is some friend allowing you to use it?'

'Strictly speaking the jet belongs to Valiente Capital, the Spanish investment firm. I am the CEO of Valiente Capital. That I also paint is a secret, a diversion from my normal life as a hedge-fund manager and I use the pseudonym V for my portraits to conserve that privacy,' Ruy explained with cool precision.

Investment, hedge funds? Suzy's brain swam. She would probably have been less taken aback had he announced that he was a bullfighter. But some sort of financial wizard? That was so far removed from what she had so far seen of Ruy that she was wildly disconcerted, and then her thoughts took a step back and she recalled that cool, arrogant side to his nature. 'Why weren't you honest with me about who you were from the start?' she demanded tightly.

'My two identities are kept very much separate and few people know the truth. Cecile is one of the few. I'm not sure our investors would be happy to learn that I'm an artist as well. I bought the house in England as a bolt-hole where I could paint when I take time off and I see no reason to tell anyone that I'm also involved in the financial markets.'

'How rich *are* you?' Suzy shot at him thinly, an unpleasant thought suddenly occurring to her. 'Rich enough to have paid me that fifty thousand pounds I mentioned that night in the pub and think nothing of it?'

Steady dark eyes with only a gleam of gold in their depths rested on her as Ruy compressed his lips and jerked his chin in confirmation.

'And I laughed and asked if you thought you were Mr Rockefeller or something!' Suzy recalled with a shudder of humiliation, her cheeks burning. 'You've had a lot of fun at my expense!'

'What's that supposed to mean?' Ruy countered, taken aback by the charge.

'I may not have the right to know your secrets, but I *did* have the right to know the identity and status of the man I slept with. I was entitled to be told who you really were *before* that happened,' Suzy condemned. 'Because I can tell you right now that if I'd known you were some flash hedge-fund whizz-kid, I wouldn't have gone to bed with you in the first place!'

'Why the hell not? What possible difference could it have made?' Ruy slammed back at her, angry for the first time in her presence, thoroughly nettled by that word, 'flash', which seemed to suggest that he was some sort of untrustworthy braggart.

'I don't even know your real name!' Suzy yelled back at him above the roar of the engines as the jet rolled down the runway.

'Ruy Santiago Valiente,' Ruy supplied with icy precision. 'Rivera was Cecile's mother's surname and I borrow it when I don't wish to be identified.'

'How convenient to have an alternative name!' Suzy snapped between clenched teeth of scorn.

Ruy exhaled slowly, cocked an ebony brow and murmured, 'I really don't see what the problem is. I've told you now.'

Suzy gripped her right hand with her left because she wanted to hit him. 'You deceived me. You betrayed my trust.'

'Those are serious accusations,' Ruy bit out, his temper stirring even more.

'And they're *true*. You didn't give me a choice. I feel like an idiot for not seeing that, the way you behaved, you couldn't possibly have been the forthright artist you were pretending to be!'

Ruy gritted his teeth. 'Most women would be ecstatic to find out that I'm a wealthy man.'

Suzy's hands both flew up in the air to emphasise her furious frustration with him and his refusal to look at the situation from her point of view. 'If they're greedy, if they want you to spend your money on them, but I don't! Now I can see that you've used your wealth like a weapon against me from the moment we met!' she framed with bitter resentment.

The jet was finally in the air and Ruy released his seat belt and vaulted upright to his full intimidating height. He stared down at her with scorching dark golden eyes. *'Valgame Dios!* How do you make that out?'

Suzy released her belt and got up as well, moving away several feet before spinning back round to face him. 'You tried to bribe me.'

'And it would have worked a treat had you known who I was at the time because you were desperate to save your father and his livelihood,' Ruy reminded her drily.

Suzy stamped a pompommed toe. 'That is not the point!'

'That is exactly the point. Everything has turned out very well for you and your father...*why?*' Ruy prompted expectantly, as if he were a teacher giving a young, not very bright child a lesson in life. 'Because I have money, and I was able to use that money you deride to protect you and your father from further interference and intimidation from Brenton. Don't you dare snipe at me for telling you the truth you don't want to hear or accept!'

As Suzy angrily parted her lips the cabin door opened and a stewardess appeared. Deeply flushed, Suzy backed down into her seat again and sat there frozen in place while refreshments and snacks were served. She was so angry she was trembling with the force of her feelings. On one level she knew that Ruy was right. He *had* saved the pub from her ex's machinations. He *had* made her father's life a lot easier by releasing him from years of worry about money. But, ultimately, she was convinced that Ruy had bought into the pub to ensure that Suzy agreed to model for him and accompanied him out to Spain to pose as his fiancée.

'Yes, what you did may have delivered a happy result for my father, but it doesn't change the unscrupulous way you operate. You bought into the pub to put pressure on me.'

'I bought into the pub to take pressure *off* you,' Ruy stressed curtly.

'I had the right to know your true identity before I slept with you,' Suzy sliced back at him sharply.

'It was casual sex, Suzy…not a life-changing choice!' Ruy raked back at her cuttingly.

Her face flamed at the wounding reminder. What had meant a great deal to her had meant considerably less to him and that hurt, yes, it did, no matter how hard she resented that reality. Ruy had lied to her and that scared her and made her very wary, particularly after she had innocently chosen to trust Percy. She had already suffered the knowledge that she was not that perfect a judge of character and she knew she needed to be more careful.

'Yes, it worked out so well for you when you ended up bedding a stalker!' Suzy reminded him helplessly, needled by the statement that their encounter had been casual on his terms when it had been anything but casual for her when he had become her first lover.

A muscle pulled taut at the corner of Ruy's unsmiling mouth. 'You slept with me because you wanted me. It would have been wrong had I been married or concealing some other relevant fact that you needed to know, but I *wasn't.*'

'I wouldn't have chosen to become intimate with a guy so far removed from my own world!' Suzy retorted fiercely.

'That's inverse snobbery,' Ruy countered, marvelling at the stubborn manner in which she held onto her ire, refusing to be soothed or to accept that he had done nothing wrong.

'No, it's not. You're rich and I should've worked that out for myself because you don't really hide it that well. You're very arrogant. You think you can buy whatever you want and that your wishes and needs are more important than other people's. You rearranged my life and my father's purely to suit yourself.'

'It suited you as well,' Ruy incised coolly,

all logic and calm, which only increased the frustrated rage she was suppressing.

'Oh, shut up!' Suzy finally launched at him in exasperation, ramming down the hurt feelings tugging at her that he was *not* the man she had naively assumed he was. Once again, she had made the wrong judgement call and that scared her. 'I've heard enough of your smooth, specious arguments. You could probably talk your way out of murder but I'm not listening any more!'

And with that ultimate strike, Suzy rose from her seat, swiped up the magazines the stewardess had brought her and stalked to the end of that section of cabin to sit out of his view. Ruy brooded on his rage, even white teeth gritted. He was very wealthy, he had always been wealthy, and he supposed a certain level of arrogance and selfishness afflicted most men in his position. He was accustomed to getting his own way. He was used to paying more to get it too, it being his experience that those he dealt with *expected* him to pay more because he could afford it. How was that wrong?

What difference did his status in life make to her? Would she honestly have rejected him had she known that he was rich? And why was she the very first woman in his life to fight with him over the reality that he was as rich as Midas? The first woman to criticise him…aside of Cecile. And his sister adored him and only offered occasional nuggets of unwelcome truth in an effort to improve his character.

'I have a business call to make,' Ruy informed her as he came to a halt in the archway next to her seat. 'But before I leave, allow me to have the final word.'

Suzy lifted her head, green eyes glittering like emeralds, soft pink mouth flattening with tension.

'You had sex with me for the same reason I had sex with you, *querida*,' he imparted softly.

'Which was…?' Suzy dared, enraged by the heat she could feel hotly flooding her cheeks.

'*Hombre!* Reason had nothing to do with it. We were so hot for each other we couldn't control ourselves. At least I'm honest about it,' Ruy told her mockingly.

CHAPTER SEVEN

As THE LIMOUSINE that collected Ruy and Suzy from the airport pulled away from the kerb, the silence within the vehicle was frigid. Suzy played with her phone and did everything she could to avoid looking in Ruy's direction while he passed his time with business calls, switching with enviable ease between several different languages. Having no idea exactly where they were heading and still too angry with Ruy to ask, Suzy was exasperated with both him and herself by the time the limo turned off a rural road to move up a long straight driveway. The lane was bounded by tall dark cypress trees that cast spear-shaped shadows across the pale sunlit gravel.

A gargantuan building came into view at the top of the drive. The substantial house in the centre was extended on either side by wings. It was a mansion, composed of several storeys and countless windows.

'Welcome to Palacio Valiente,' Ruy murmured as the limousine drove below an archway and came to a halt in a cobbled interior courtyard, adorned with a marble fountain.

An arched veranda with polished floor tiles ringed the entire space. Elegant urns of colourful flowers tumbled from every corner. Suzy climbed slowly out of the car. A hand lightly cupping her elbow, Ruy moved forward to greet the small middle-aged man awaiting them. They moved indoors down a short corridor into a vast echoing marble entrance hall in which life-sized classical statues stood in niches.

'Manuel is scolding me for bringing you into the house for the first time by the rear entrance,' Ruy told her with amusement. 'He manages the staff and the household—'

Suzy was still in shock at the size and style of Ruy's home while telling herself that she should have guessed by his attitude that he would live in a literal palace. How he had accommodated his pedigreed expectations to that relatively small, if spacious, house in Norfolk she had no idea because by his standards he had been roughing it. Ruy had not only grown up with the proverbial silver spoon, he had grown up with an entire silver canteen. The entrance hall was cool, splendid and thoroughly intimidating, designed, she felt, to remind less high-flown mortals of their lowlier place in life.

A sweeping staircase that split in two higher up to curve in opposite directions sat before her. Suzy thought in sudden horror, *Oh, my goodness, my clothes just aren't going to cut it here!* He had said a high-society wedding, but she had seriously underestimated the level of glitz and expense that would be expected. And once again that was all *his* fault for not being more honest. He had worn an elegant business suit to travel home, she had put on cropped trousers and a tee and that contrast said it all.

Ruy thrust open the door of a room off the

landing and stood back. Her delicate profile tight, she moved ahead of him into a breathtakingly magnificent bedroom. A superb canopied and draped ornate bed sat at the far end of the room. 'This looks like somewhere royalty would sleep,' she whispered uneasily, feeling as if she should be standing behind a rope reading a guidebook on some official tour.

'No, this is where we sleep,' Ruy countered.

'We?' Suzy almost gasped.

'It may be an old house but expectations here are as contemporary as anywhere else. Engaged couples share a bed,' Ruy informed her smoothly.

'Even when they're barely speaking?'

'Particularly in that case. Never let the sun go down on anger,' Ruy quipped.

'Any more clichés to offer?' Suzy was playing for time because back in England she had become accustomed to having a bed to herself. Ruy had stayed in his studio, she had stayed upstairs. After their fleeting bout of intimacy, that division, that privacy, had provided a welcome escape from the turmoil of emotions Ruy's presence incited inside her. But whether she liked it or not, he was correct in his assertion that people would expect an engaged couple to share a room.

Ruy crossed the room to tug open a door onto a balcony. 'I want you to put on the feather dress and your boots and I'll meet you down…there.' He indicated the wrought-iron staircase that ran down to the charming inner courtyard below them.

'It's an orange grove,' she whispered in recognition, gazing down on the plump fruit bright against the rich evergreen leaves of the trees.

'Yes… I'll get changed. I don't usually paint here but for you I will make an exception. After all, there is no one alive now who cares what I do,' Ruy breathed abstractedly, dark shadowed eyes lightening as he glanced up at the azure-blue sky above. 'I should celebrate that freedom whenever I can.'

Her luggage and his arrived while Suzy was still mulling over his words and trying to fathom why he had sounded both regretful and energised. A maid appeared to tackle her cases and Suzy quickly lifted the feather dress in its garment bag and her boots and vanished into the bathroom to dress in private. As she descended the outside steps into the courtyard the intoxicating sultry scent of the oranges rose in the midday heat.

A few minutes later Ruy strode down the stairs, his attention welded to the slender silhouette of Suzy standing in the white dress beneath the trees. In that instant, reality and fantasy smoothly merged into a perfect whole for him. He directed her down onto the worn stone bench below one of the trees and arranged her in a sideways pose, one booted foot braced on the bench, the other on the ground, her face turned towards him, her riot of vibrant copper curls spiralling round her slight shoulders, slender legs edged with a jagged white feather hem. With her luminous skin warmed to a hint of a soft pink glow by the heat, she looked utterly amazing.

Suzy studied Ruy as he sank down opposite her. She had no other choice when she was not permitted to move her head. In his suit he had looked sleek and sophisticated and distant. In well-worn jeans and a shirt, he looked overwhelmingly masculine and somehow rougher and sexier round the edges with dark stubble outlining his hard jawline and accentuating his wide, sensual mouth. Her body clenched as she remembered the taste of him, the pounding urgency of his lean, hard body on hers. A very slight shudder slivered through her, her nipples pinching taut, her skin prickling with that unstoppable tide of awareness and tightening her flesh round her bones.

A phone was buzzing. It had to be his because he ignored it, ebony brows flaring in annoyance. A door opened nearby. Manuel appeared, wringing his hands apologetically and imparting the message that someone just wouldn't take no for an answer. Ruy swore under his breath and tossed aside the sketch pad. He dug out his phone, stabbed buttons, paced away before swinging back to her to take a photo of her and that particular pose. 'We'll have to call it a day. I have to go into the office. Feel free to explore.'

'I will.' Suzy rose slowly and straightened her stiff muscles. She was hungry and thirsty and tired but determined to make the most of her freedom. She climbed the stairs and unzipped the dress, removing it to drape it over a chair arm. She kicked off the boots and pressed her warm feet against the relief of the cold tiled floor before going for a shower. Her clothes had been neatly put away for her in the cabinets and wardrobes in the same room that Ruy had used. She pulled out shorts and a vest top, more suitable for the heat. Manuel was waiting for her when she came downstairs to usher her into a wonderfully air-conditioned room and serve her with a beautiful salad while offering to show her round the *palacio* after her meal.

Ruy couldn't settle at work. He dealt with the minor crisis that had erupted but his laser-sharp concentration swiftly evaporated. He looked several times at the photo of Suzy on his phone and wondered what she was doing, grimly amused by his wandering thoughts. Of course, he was always driven and obsessed in the first fine flush with a new model, a new painting, he reminded himself. His fascination would ebb once he had finally contrived to pin down and capture Suzy's effervescent spirit on canvas.

His sexual fascination? That, he sensed, might be another story because that was without precedent. He paced his office, wondering why that hunger refused to quit. One and done was his pattern. He took a woman for one night and treated her like a queen for that night but there were no repeats, no extended interludes. He didn't get involved in relationships. He had tried a couple of times, but within the space of a handful of dates the women concerned would get on his nerves and begin assuming that they were more important to him than they were and then he had to let them down gently. In truth, he didn't like hurting people, women in particular, and

some individuals, like Liliana, were dangerously fragile. It was easier simply to stick
to one-night stands. Nobody misunderstood
what was on offer then and nobody got hurt.

But, unfortunately, one experience of Suzy
hadn't been enough to satisfy him. He hadn't
even got a whole night with her. And worst
of all, every moment of that impulsive, hasty
encounter was etched on his mind like a scar.
From her point of view, it must have been
a pretty poor introduction to sex and that
dented his ego and shamed him, but he hadn't
known, couldn't have guessed that she would
be that innocent. Even so, he didn't believe
that let him off the hook. And now he would
never have the chance to show her how different it could be. After her experience with
her ex and then his own callous words in the
aftermath, the last thing Suzy needed now
was another man trying to put pressure on
her. He had promised that he wouldn't do
that. He had to keep that promise.

Ruy arrived home in time for dinner and
found Suzy in the long portrait gallery with

Manuel. Manuel was carefully naming pieces of antique furniture in Spanish and correcting Suzy's pronunciation while giving her a potted history of the characters in the portraits. As most of them had led lives of stultifying boredom, Ruy was surprised to hear her laughter ring out. He was already trying not to let his gaze linger too long on her long shapely legs in denim shorts and the perky tilt of her unbound breasts or even the glorious messy tumble of her curls. That silvery peal of laughter only energised the throb at his groin.

'Ruy!' she exclaimed when she noticed him, tall and dark and devastatingly handsome in his silvery grey designer suit.

Manuel smiled and left them alone.

'Poor Manuel,' Suzy sighed. 'He thinks you're going to marry me and so he's trying to get my Spanish up to speed and educate me about your home and your ancestors.'

'My family were bankers to royalty for centuries. That's just about all you need to know. What made you laugh?'

'The one who had a whole string of wives,' Suzy confided, an irrepressible twinkle in her bright eyes. 'Your family's version of Henry the Eighth.'

'Except Diego's five unfortunate wives died in childbirth,' Ruy explained.

'I suppose back then that was very common,' Suzy remarked thoughtfully. 'Thank goodness it isn't now.'

'My mother died in childbirth and my baby sister with her,' Ruy heard himself admit in argument, startled to hear himself proffering that confidence, but there was something in the freedom with which she spoke and behaved with him that smashed his usual reserve and brought his own barriers crashing down. Somehow she made him *want* to tell her stuff and he couldn't explain that to his own satisfaction. 'It's less common, but it still happens.'

'What age were you?'

'Rigo and I were five. Our world fell apart without her. She was very loving. My father, on the other hand, was more of a "spare the rod and spoil the child" parent.'

'I'm so sorry. At least I was too young to be aware of my loss and Dad was very caring.'

'You were fortunate. Our father didn't have a kind bone in his body. He punished my brother and I for the smallest infraction. I excelled at school, but I still got punished for not doing well enough to please. Rigo, regrettably, was not academic. As you can imagine, he suffered more,' Ruy told her grimly. 'My father made Rigo compete with me and never let him forget that I was the elder, the heir, the *important* son. It destroyed our relationship.'

'So, you were never close to your twin?'

'No. He grew up resenting me and that never went away…in our twenties, something occurred that destroyed any hope of a closer relationship.'

'And what was that?' Suzy prompted, hungry for more detail, conscious that Ruy rarely spoke so freely with her.

'Rigo was addicted to drugs for a while. I

don't wish to share his history,' Ruy admitted very stiffly. 'That is his business.'

Suzy reddened, aware that she had asked one question too many and mortified as she took a determined step back from that angle. 'What was it like for Cecile?' she asked.

'Cecile's mother was my father's mistress. She didn't grow up with us and he never officially acknowledged her as his daughter. Rigo wants nothing to do with her because according to him accepting Cecile into the family is dissing my father's memory. Even though our father was cruel to him, he still regards him as the ultimate standard of what he should aspire to.'

'Life's too short for an outlook like that.' Suzy sighed ruefully, passing by him into the bedroom, relieved to have finished that conversation and backed away from it. 'Do I need to change for dinner or anything?'

'Not for my benefit, particularly when you look as incredible as you do in those shorts,' Ruy told her with a slow smile.

Her face went pink as she watched him remove his jacket and tug his tie loose. The little intimacies of a shared room tugged uneasily at her and she walked restlessly over to the window. 'Is that orange grove in the courtyard the one you were referring to?'

'Yes, but there's another wilder, larger version of it at the far end of the gardens beside the estate orchards. I remember playing hide and seek there as a child,' Ruy imparted, his voice closer than she expected.

Suzy whirled round and there he was, a couple of feet away, clad only in boxers, almost every inch of his magnificent body bare for her perusal. Involuntarily her eyes roamed over the expanse of his bronzed torso, lingering on the corrugated slab of his abs and flat stomach. Her mouth ran dry, her tongue glued to the roof of her mouth.

'Don't look at me like that. I'm not good at self-denial,' Ruy warned her.

'Neither am I,' Suzy croaked, noticing, well, she really couldn't help noticing that he was aroused. Those boxers didn't hide much. 'How was I looking at you?'

'Like you want me…like I look at you,' Ruy framed hoarsely. *'Dios mio!* Even my grammar's going to hell!'

Warmth mushroomed inside Suzy at the confirmation that he still wanted her but that, just like her, he was in conflict over it. Still being tempted by him had seemed weak until he made that same admission. 'I was so angry with you this morning…still am, because you aren't the guy I thought you were and that threw me…and now I don't have the right clothes.'

'I'll get you more clothes,' Ruy swore impatiently. 'Little problems of that sort aren't important.'

'You're not allowed to buy me anything more,' Suzy reminded him. 'You keep your money to yourself.'

Ruy reached out and closed his big hands round her smaller ones to tug her closer. 'Anything you want. I need you to be happy.'

'It doesn't take money to make me happy,' Suzy mumbled. 'Well, except when it came to saving Dad from Percy.'

'There's an exception to every rule,' Ruy conceded generously while stilling in the act of edging her even closer. 'We're not supposed to be doing this.'

'That's your rule,' Suzy pointed out helplessly.

And he kissed her, and a long breathless sigh of relief escaped her. The tension holding her fast snapped and propelled her into the muscular heat of him, her hands sliding up to his shoulders and stretching round his neck, her entire body melting and pliant. 'I want you,' she whispered daringly. 'But not if you're liable to freak out afterwards.'

'Absolutely no freaking out,' Ruy swore raggedly half under his breath. 'Are you sure about this? I'm still the same guy who doesn't want a relationship.'

'Do we have to put a label on it? I don't want a relationship right now either, not after escaping Percy. Do you think you could go with the flow just for once?' Suzy murmured softly as she backed him towards the bed.

An unholy grin lit Ruy's lean dark features

as he realised what she was doing. 'Just for once,' he agreed, angling his lean hips against her, further acquainting her with his arousal.

A kernel of pure exhilaration, unlike anything Suzy had ever felt before, sparked and glowed at the heart of her, igniting an impatient pulse of need. He tugged her down on the bed and kissed her until she was pushing up against him, eager for more. She was with him every step of the way. He extracted her from her top, teased the pouting tips of her breasts and buried his mouth there to take advantage of her passionate response before beginning to remove her shorts. Her body felt as though it was already racing ahead of her, taut and trembling with seething anticipation.

'You'd run away if you knew the things I want to do to you,' Ruy growled against the slender column of her white throat, his mouth nipping along the tender slope of her neck, making her squirm and gasp while he delicately stroked and traced the damp triangle of cloth stretched between her thighs.

Her heart was racing at an insane level. It

was a crazy challenge simply to catch her breath. Sheer physical excitement had gripped her in an unbreakable hold. He peeled her out of her last garment. The burn at her core was relentless, tiny ripples of tension already ringing her pelvis and building in demand. He spread her trembling legs, lowered his head and used his tongue on her tender flesh while he eased a finger into her. Irresistible sensation engulfed Suzy in a heady wave and a rosy flush warmed her entire skin surface as she rocked her slender hips. Erotic bliss, a whole world of sensual extremes, captured her and wrung powerful responses from her sensitised body. Flung up to an ecstatic height that made her cry out, she felt fireworks flare through her entire being and light her up until she fell back against the pillows to marvel at the tiny convulsions of pure pleasure still currenting through her.

Her shimmering green eyes locked to him. She lifted a feathery copper brow. 'You're allowed to shock and awe me in bed,' she con-

ceded with deadly seriousness and no small
amount of complacency.

After a disconcerted pause, Ruy flung himself back on the bed and laughed with raw
appreciation. No other woman had ever given
him such a sense of freedom. He reared back
up again to crush her parted lips under his
and let his tongue delve deep, that carnal kiss
reawakening the sensual hum deep inside her.
'*Dios*... I'm burning up for you,' he told her
hoarsely.

He reached for protection, carefully rearranged her supple body and plunged into
her hard and fast. Her back arched, her hips
rose, a formless sound of need quivering from
her lips. His fierce rhythm sent compelling
surges of delight through her and the excitement climbed, little paroxysms of convul-
sive sensual heat tying her into a tight knot
of anticipation until the pleasure rose to an
uncontrollable height, loosened the knot of
need and blew her away again.

'See...no freak out,' Ruy breathed huskily
in the aftermath, gazing down with smoul-

dering dark golden eyes at her hectically flushed face.

'The earth definitely moved,' Suzy told him with dancing eyes of admiration as she smoothed a possessive hand down over his heaving ribcage. 'Do you think you can keep that standard up for a whole week?'

'A week...why only a week?' An immediate frown tensed Ruy's lean dark features.

'Because I'm only here for a week,' Suzy reminded him cheerfully.

Ruy unclenched his taut jawline and thought about it. A week was a very long time for him with a woman. In fact, he had never spent that much time or that many nights with one particular woman. The sex was spectacular but that could possibly be a mere side effect of his artistic obsession with her. By the time he completed his sketches and started to paint her, he would probably be far too preoccupied by his art to care too much about her departure.

Ruy closed an arm round her. 'I intend to make the most of this week.'

And so did Suzy, lying there dreamily compliant in her sensual daze. She would make the most of Ruy and her trip to Spain and then return to her normal life. A life in which she would make changes, she planned reflectively with a little leap of anticipation that for once had nothing to do with Ruy. If her father no longer needed her to work at the pub, she would be free to decide her own future and there were a dizzying number of options available. Although perhaps there weren't quite so many options open to someone like her without higher-level education, she acknowledged ruefully. Perhaps the first move she would have to make would be signing up to study towards better qualifications.

'What are you thinking about?' Ruy pressed, sensing her abstraction and irritated by it.

'Going home,' she told him truthfully.

His brilliant dark eyes glittered like polished jet. At that moment he didn't want her thinking about anything but him, and the very strangeness of that thought disconcerted him.

It was because that desire of hers to return

home put pressure on him to complete the painting, he reasoned uneasily. And possibly just a little because he wanted her full attention to be on him—and that was normal, wasn't it? Particularly for a guy who had never had to fight for a woman's attention before...

OK, Ruy thought with sudden ferocity, *challenge accepted.*

CHAPTER EIGHT

'DON'T MOVE YOUR HAND,' Ruy instructed. 'And, no, don't twist your face up like that. You're a creature of perpetual motion, *querida*. You must learn how to sit still.'

'Were you like this as a kid?' Suzy queried impatiently. 'Did you make your friends sit like statues while you drew them?'

'My friends didn't know about my artistic propensities.'

Suzy studied him intently, taking in the gleaming black hair, the proud high cheekbones, the dark deep-set eyes that flashed gold in sunlight or emotion. He was gorgeous, particularly when dressed down to paint in worn jeans and a tee that showcased every inch of his lean, beautifully muscular body. The sensuality of that thought brought colour to her cheeks but six days of pretty much constant intimacy with Ruy had wrecked her ability to step back and maintain her cool. Now she looked at him and her own body clenched and throbbed in reaction even though she ached from their mutual enthusiasm.

'And why was that?'

'My father punished me for drawing or for showing any interest in art.'

'But *why*?' she exclaimed in disbelief.

'My father's younger brother, Lorenzo, was an artist. He was also defiantly gay. My father was a bigot and he cut his brother out of his life, but he grew up associating any kind of artistic leanings in a man with homosexuality. My desire to draw horrified him and he tried to beat it out of me.'

'That's appalling!' Suzy gasped in shock at his calm manner of talking about such inhumane treatment.

'I learned to hide my interest at an early age,' Ruy admitted, his sensual mouth quirking. 'But, perhaps, Armando *was* rather unlucky with his sons. Rodrigo, after all, has a similar creative streak. He's become a successful art dealer and is the owner of a fashionable art gallery in Seville. This *palacio* is, after all, the home of one of the most valuable private art collections in Spain, consisting of paintings assembled over many hundreds of years by my ancestors. Art and collecting is in our blood.'

Her smooth brow furrowed. 'Your father sounds like a monster. Is that why you keep your artistic side a big secret?'

Ruy's strong jawline clenched. 'It was the start of it, certainly. I wasn't strong enough to fight my father off and stop those punishments of his until I was a teenager and by then a lot of damage had been done and the secrecy had become a habit.'

'Your brother must know about your art,' Suzy assumed.

'No, he doesn't, and I must ask you to remember not to mention it to anyone at the wedding tomorrow,' Ruy warned her grimly.

'You know I won't if you don't want me to,' Suzy told him soothingly. 'But why is it *still* a secret? Why do you feel the need to hide such an important part of yourself from the rest of the world?'

Ruy had never asked himself that question, which struck him as an odd glaring omission. 'Custom, privacy,' he responded. 'For many years, it felt like the only thing in my life that was truly mine and I guarded my secret zealously.'

'Would you give up Valiente Capital to paint full-time?' Suzy asked.

'No,' Ruy answered without hesitation. 'Once I believed that, given the choice, I would do that, but since then I've come to appreciate that I also very much enjoy the cut and thrust of the financial world. I think that's in my genes as much as the need to paint.' He set down his palette. 'That will do us for today. Manuel is providing a picnic lunch for us. I did promise to show you the estate.'

'I thought you'd forgotten… I want to see the orange grove where you used to hide.'

Ruy closed a hand over hers as she rose

and tottered slightly on her stiff limbs. His other hand winding into her curls, he drew her slight frame up against him. The heat of his skin and the aroma of clean, fresh male engulfed her and the pulse at the heart of her quickened. The strength of the hunger Ruy ignited in her unnerved her because she had never thought of herself as a particularly sexual being and now she was learning that she hadn't known herself as well as she thought she did. Her nipples prickled and peaked and her body dampened, her pupils dilating.

'Sometimes I want to eat you alive,' Ruy groaned hungrily against her ripe mouth. 'I thought this would fade...*why* isn't it fading?'

'Feed a cold, starve a fever,' she framed shakily. 'Maybe you were right and we shouldn't be doing this.'

'*Que pasa?* What's the matter with you?' Ruy growled, ravishing her parted lips passionately with his own in punishment for that suggestion, his tongue delving deep enough to make her shudder against him as if she were in the teeth of a gale. 'This is us. *This is how it is.*'

But she felt consumed by him, by the passion she couldn't deny, by the boundaries she couldn't make herself respect. He walked her indoors to the air-conditioned cool but still she felt as though her skin had shrunk too tight over her bones and her heartbeat was pounding as if she had run a mile. Ruy wanted to lift her up into his arms and stride upstairs with her, but instead he forced himself to stay in control with her simply to prove that he could do it...*this once.*

Manuel was beaming at them from a discreet corner. They were definitely putting on an authentic show of being lovers, Ruy acknowledged without the satisfaction he had expected to feel. She would be leaving in a day and a half, straight after the wedding. He already knew that he would miss her. Not just the passion, but the new life she brought to the *palacio.*

A huge bunch of sunflowers gathered from the edge of a field by Suzy sat in a giant vase on a table, transforming the splendid marble hall into a much warmer space. Suzy cast a kind of spell over the old house, changing practices that had been in vogue for decades. A cardigan she had abandoned over a carved chair provided another splash of colour. She could be rather untidy, Ruy conceded, because he had tripped over the boots she'd left lying on the bedroom floor the night before. Not that on the way into a bed containing Suzy he had felt remotely tempted to complain.

They now ate their meals in the airy orangery, not in the formal dining room, where she had confessed to feeling oppressed by the heavy tapestries on the wall and the giant table. She had taken a notion for fish and chips one afternoon and had casually suggested it to Manuel and, lo and behold, Ruy's *cordon bleu* chef had served fish and chips for the first time ever and had then emerged from the kitchens he ruled like a tyrant to enquire as to whether she had any other special requests. Informed that Suzy loved to be surprised, the chef had grinned and Ruy had appreciated that his regimented menu of meals—for *he* did *not* like to be surprised by what was on his plate—would be changed for ever. Suzy smiled and said thank you and the staff couldn't do enough for her.

On the landing he succumbed to the allure of her soft pink mouth and crushed her to him to extract a hungry kiss. They walked into his bedroom and Suzy stopped dead. Ruy frowned at the display of rails holding a wide selection of women's clothes.

'What's all this?'

'You said you weren't sure that your clothes were what you needed for your stay here or for the wedding. I ordered a selection of designer garments in your sizes. I'm sorry I forgot to mention it,' he completed truthfully as he closed a hand over hers. 'You can look at them later.'

'Ruy,' she muttered in frustration. 'For goodness' sake, I'm leaving soon!'

'I thought you could donate them to a charity afterwards,' Ruy suggested, feeling quite pleased with that community-minded advice. 'Or even auction them off for a good cause.'

Suzy gritted her teeth at the prospect of garments so expensive that it would be worth auctioning them and groaned. 'I tell you not to be sneaky and you just get *sneakier*!' she complained. 'And what's in that giant chest sitting on the dressing table?'

Ruy shrugged. 'Some jewellery I had Manuel take out of the vault. It belongs to my family and it's overdue an airing. If you don't want new clothes, I can guarantee that festooning yourself in diamonds that haven't been seen in a couple of generations will work as an alternative. Nobody will look beyond the Valiente jewels.'

Suzy sucked in much-needed oxygen. Ruy caught her fingers in his again.

'Stop trying to distract me,' she warned him. 'And unzip this dress.'

Ruy watched her peel off the dress, her slender but delicately curved body emerging from the feathered folds. She kicked off the boots. He automatically toed them out of the way beneath a chair. Wearing only bra and panties, Suzy vanished into the dressing room and appeared mere minutes later in a casual yellow sundress, standing on one foot in the doorway and then on the other as she donned canvas sneakers.

Suzy watched him watching her, tensing as her mouth ran dry and her heart thumped with the excitement she couldn't suppress. Ruy might often infuriate her but she knew that she was falling in love with him in a very big way. Nobody had ever made her feel as he did and very probably nobody would ever make her feel that way again. The hours she spent with Ruy raced by at supersonic speed because he fascinated her. His sheer passionate intensity enthralled her and had given her back the confidence that Percy had stolen from her, because it was impossible to feel like a lesser being with a guy like Ruy, who could not hide his desire and appreciation from her. He wasn't just lethally attractive and insanely sexy, he was clever and entertaining and complex. The more she got to know him, the more she wanted to know. But she also knew that their time together was fast running out and that she wouldn't figure in his future except as a girl he had once painted.

Suzy wasn't fanciful and she didn't believe in miracles. She knew that Ruy viewed her as an enjoyable fling and nothing more. He had warned her that he didn't have relationships as such with women and she had listened, but her heart and her body had overruled her common sense. She had given in to temptation. She had honestly believed that she could stop her emotions getting too deeply involved but that had proved to be a naïve hope. Now she knew that heartbreak loomed on her horizon. She had been too trusting, too confident in her assumption that she could protect herself and too ignorant of how intimacy could change and strengthen everything between a man and a woman.

Even so, she wasn't one to cry over spilt milk and she didn't think that she had any true regrets. She couldn't say that she wished that she had never met Ruy because she had revelled in every high and low of being with him. She was almost twenty-two years old and he was the first man in her life—she didn't count Percy. At her age, it was normal to succumb to physical attraction and hope that it would develop into something deeper. It was equally normal to fall in love and get hurt. She would learn to live with the disappointment, she told herself fiercely.

Ruy answered his phone and began to talk in Spanish. It was his sister, Cecile, and Suzy saw him frown and start to pace as the conversation heated up. After several strained responses when she could clearly see that he was hanging onto his temper by a thread, the call ended.

'I'm afraid I'll have to ask you to remain one full day longer after the wedding.'

Her brow furrowed. 'Why?'

'Cecile was phoning to warn me that my family are throwing an engagement party here for us the day after Rigo's wedding,' he explained. 'Manuel refused to make any arrangements without the go-ahead from me, which is why Cecile has shared their plans in advance.'

'No, I can't stay any longer,' Suzy interrupted worriedly, keen to stick to the timetable initially agreed between them.

'Would you really leave me to face an engagement party without a fiancée?' Ruy demanded in astonishment.

Suzy reddened. 'What's the point? I'll be leaving and disappearing from your life soon anyway.'

'*One* day,' Ruy emphasised, dark golden eyes brilliant. 'We're talking about one day. Why are you in such a hurry to get home?'

'Because I've got plans,' Suzy responded with determined cheer. 'Dad doesn't need me working at the pub any more. I'd like to work with children in the future and I'm going to look into studying towards that goal. I'll need to get applications in now if I want to get onto a course.'

'One more day, *querida*,' Ruy murmured

drily. 'Don't make it a big deal. I didn't ask for this party either.'

Suzy sucked in a sustaining breath, wanting to be fair and yet resenting him for putting pressure on her. 'I'll agree because it would be unreasonable to say no in the circumstances, but no is really what you deserve...' She waved a meaningful hand at the racks of clothing and the antique box of jewellery. 'You constantly chip away at what I want to try and turn it into what *you* want instead. I don't like that.'

The faintest colour edged Ruy's sculpted cheekbones. 'I enjoy smoothing out problems for you, solving them,' he argued as he moved forward. 'You're letting me paint you. You're faking being my betrothed for my benefit. I owe you and I like to pay my debts.'

'Some things in life are free, Ruy,' Suzy declared, her pulses pounding at the smouldering glitter in his gaze. 'You don't owe me anything and I don't owe you anything either. Let's keep this simple.'

'You want me to return the clothes?' he prompted tautly.

'Not until I've picked out something suitable for a fancy engagement party,' Suzy responded with a rueful roll of her bright eyes. 'And now Cecile knows about our pretend engagement as well.'

'Cecile knows the truth…that you're doing me a favour,' Ruy contradicted.

'Like I'm about to complain about a week in a palace abroad where I'm being waited on hand and foot!' Suzy quipped, flashing him a look of amusement, needing to come across as light-hearted and fully aware that nothing between them was real or lasting. 'And the sex isn't bad either.'

'Cheeky,' Ruy remarked with a sizzling smile, reaching for her and discovering that at the very last minute she wasn't there any more.

'Lunch,' she reminded him from the bedroom door. 'I'm starving!'

She would keep it light and chirpy right up until the moment she departed. She wasn't the clingy, needy type and, worse, he would be repelled by any hint of clinginess after suffering the attentions of a stalker in the past. No, there would be no behaviour of that nature on her part. She would laugh and she would smile, and she would stay normal and buoyant right to the bitter end.

CHAPTER NINE

'YOU LOOK FANTASTIC,' Ruy murmured as Suzy emerged from the dressing room, a flirty net fascinator anchored in her vibrant curls. She was an amazingly sexy vision. No man in the world would wonder why he was with such a beauty. That emerald-green shade accentuated her translucent skin and vibrant curls.

Her elegant gown, with its strategic panelled splits, revealed an occasional discreet flash of long shapely calf and tiny feet shod in high-heeled shoes that were a curious mix of bondage boot and sandal, with narrow straps that bared her toes while accentuating the delicacy of her ankles. 'I notice that you're not wearing any jewellery.'

'I'm wearing the engagement ring, but I decided it was best not to borrow anything from that chest,' Suzy told him gently. 'I'm not a member of the family and it would be tasteless of me to be seen flaunting any of it *before* we were married. Your brother's bride would have more excuse than I would have.'

'The collection was offered to her and refused,' Ruy sliced in coolly. 'Of course, Rigo is marrying an heiress and the bride probably has her own inherited gems to flaunt.'

Suzy flushed a little. 'I wasn't being rude. I just don't think it would be appropriate for me to be showing it off in my current role. You've told me nothing about the woman your brother is marrying. Tell me more,' she urged, keen to leave the topic of the jewellery she had rejected behind.

'Her name is Mercedes Hernandez Ortega. She's the only child of a prominent industrialist and well known for her charity work. I've never met her because she's more in your age group than mine. As my father would have said, however, in a worldly sense, Rigo has done very well for himself *this* time.'

'*This* time?' she questioned as they walked downstairs.

'This is Rigo's second marriage,' Ruy admitted rather stiffly.

'He's divorced?'

'Widowed,' Ruy corrected. 'His first marriage wasn't a happy one, though.'

'Well, then, it's lovely that he's met someone else and that he wasn't soured by his first experience,' Suzy declared in that upbeat way of hers, so very different from his own more pessimistic outlook on relations between the sexes.

Ruy was almost tempted to say that his twin had been very much soured by his first marital venture and that he had put *all* the blame and responsibility for that failure squarely on his brother's shoulders. But he didn't want to talk about the past or dig up its ugly secrets, particularly not on a day when he was hoping his sibling, Rigo, had finally chosen to move on from that divisive past into a new era. That Ruy had even been invited to share his brother's big day signalled a very positive change in attitude. Even so, he would have felt a lot less comfortable attending without a woman of his own by his side.

The wedding ceremony was taking place in a huge church in Seville. It was late afternoon as they walked in the sunshine into the big building and the instant she crossed the threshold Suzy felt as if every eye in the place swivelled in her direction. A moment later she caught the whispers about *'la pelirroja'*—the redhead—and faint self-conscious colour mantled her cheeks as she sank into her seat. Ruy was a wealthy, important man in Spanish society, she reminded herself. Naturally the sudden appearance of an English fiancée, whom no one had ever met, would rouse considerable curiosity.

She studied the bridegroom waiting at the altar. Rodrigo's features were similar enough to Ruy's for Suzy to have guessed his identity, but he was less ruggedly masculine than Ruy, his build finer and he was more edgy in the fashion stakes, with his trendy-cut narrow suit and his long hair in a ponytail worn with a jewelled clasp. His bride came down the aisle in a flowing off-the-shoulder dress, her pretty face wreathed in smiles. She was a small curvy brunette with big brown eyes.

Afterwards, when Ruy greeted his brother in the crush that formed outside on the steps, Suzy immediately recognised the tension between the two men. It was there in the tightening of Rigo's mouth, the rather forced smile, and in the taut flex of Ruy's braced fingers against her spine. Ruy introduced her and she did feel as though her presence and the many questions asked of her got them all through what might have been an awkward moment. Mercedes recognised the tension as well and she was beaming and very talkative, chattering freely about her last trip to London. Suzy didn't dare tell the bride that she had only visited London twice in her entire life and that one of those occasions had been to attend a funeral. She had no knowledge whatsoever of the luxury hotel where Mercedes had stayed or of the designer shops she had enjoyed.

'How long is it since you last spoke to your brother?' Suzy asked in the limo that collected them outside the church.

'Several years,' he said stiffly.

'And how do you feel now?'

'Relieved that that first awkward meeting is over,' Ruy revealed flatly. 'I suspect I have his bride to thank for my invitation. I could see that she was very keen to stress the family connection.'

'Like me she has no siblings and she is probably struggling to understand the situation between you and Rigo.'

'I'm sure Mercedes is as well acquainted with the gossip as everyone else,' Ruy commented in a decidedly raw undertone.

Suzy stilled. 'What gossip?'

'It's nothing that you need to concern yourself with,' Ruy parried, exasperating her by putting up an immediate stone wall.

'If other people know whatever it is, shouldn't I know too?'

'If we were genuinely engaged to be married, *yes*,' Ruy agreed, cutting her to the quick with that blunt distinction. 'But as we're not, my past is not your concern.'

Painful colour flooded Suzy's face and she twisted her head away to look out of the windows at the busy streets of Seville as evening fell. Slowly the colour ebbed from her cheeks again, but she still felt quite sick at being slapped down so hard for her curiosity. Well, that was putting her in her place and no mistake, wasn't it?

Without warning, Ruy closed a hand over hers. 'I'm sorry. I'm in a filthy mood,' he breathed in a savage undertone. 'I shouldn't be taking it out on you. You deserve better from me. I simply don't want to revisit the past because what's in the past can't be changed and that frustrates me.'

Suzy snaked her fingers back from his with the instinctive recoil of hurt pride and mortification. 'That's all right. I understand,' she told him.

Ruy settled gleaming dark eyes on her in reproach. '*Please* forgive me,' he urged.

'I have.'

'No, you haven't,' Ruy contradicted. 'I know you too well to be fooled.'

But his wounding words had only reminded her that soon she would be travelling home and that Ruy and Spain and everything that had happened between them would then only be memories of a few stolen days in a world that was not her own. It hurt that he could shut her out so easily. It hurt that he wasn't willing to confide in her, even though it seemed that other people already knew that same information. It hurt to appreciate that he wasn't falling in love with her, that he would watch her walk away with the same recollections but neither the pain nor the regret that she would experience. *Well, that's the way the cookie crumbles,* she told herself sharply, *toughen up!*

'Suzy...' Ruy pressed.

'It's fine.'

'Prove it...' he breathed, releasing her seat belt and lifting her into his arms to settle her across his lap.

Suzy shivered, suddenly gathered into the

heat of him, cornered when she was striving to keep her distance, and yet she couldn't have said that she wanted him to set her free because on some level she couldn't bear to be at odds with Ruy either. 'You'll mess up my make-up.'

He pressed a button and told his driver to take the long route to Mercedes' home where the reception was being held. He ran his mouth lightly down the cord of her slender neck and inhaled deeply as her head tipped back. 'You know even the smell of your skin turns me on hard and fast. You smell delicious, like oranges in sunshine.'

'Fruity hair shampoo,' Suzy mumbled weakly, because he could make even that sound so much more romantic than reality. Ruy, she conceded, was a mass of contradictions. He said he wasn't romantic or imaginative and then he said stuff like that and made her pose in a floaty, feathery, very romantic dress in an orange grove in which only her boots cast the discordant note he seemed to like in his paintings.

He skated a teasing fingertip up the length of her thigh beneath her dress. 'I knew those slits would come in useful,' he husked.

'Ruy...*no*,' Suzy said firmly.

The fingertip flirted with the lace edge of her knickers and she snatched in a ragged breath, the promise of sensation tugging at her greedy senses while she could feel the hard thrust of his arousal beneath her. A wave of heat travelled through her entire body, leaving her weak.

One hand meshed in her curls, he ravished her parted lips with his own and every nerve ending in her body went wild with anticipation. 'Do I have a "maybe"?' he prompted thickly.

'I hope you're capable of finishing what you started,' Suzy told him starkly, her fingers meshing helplessly into his luxuriant black hair to bring his carnal mouth back to hers.

'*Hombre!* Only *you* do this to me!' Ruy growled.

'What do I do?'

'You make me desperate,' he complained,

skating skilled fingers over the tender folds at her core, discovering the damp welcome there, delicately penetrating her silken sheath, listening to her gasp and feeling her arch before retreating to a more sensitive spot that was even more responsive to his attentions.

Suzy reached a climax shatteringly fast and it left her limp, gasping against the heat and urgency of his marauding mouth, her whole body quivering with the aftershocks of pleasure. He held her close in the aftermath and breathed in slow and deep. 'I wrecked your lipstick.' He sighed. 'I'm sorry. I don't know what came over me.'

Ruy settled her down beside him again, reached for her seat belt and did it up before lifting her clutch bag from the floor and helpfully placing it on her lap. Disconcerted, Suzy glanced back at him. 'But you…er…'

'Not in the car. I draw the line at that. I'll have to wait until later,' Ruy breathed, laughing as she leant forward with a tissue to wipe his face free of her peach lipstick. 'I deserve to suffer a little.'

That quick charismatic and entirely un-inhibited smile made her want to kiss him again. Inside herself, she rebelled from that thought. Tomorrow evening, after the engagement party, she was flying home: it was arranged. It was time she forged a little distance between them and stopped throwing caution to the four winds with every kiss and every smile he gave her. Their little fling as such was almost over and he had only just finished reminding her that they *did* have boundaries, closing her out when he could have let her in...had he wanted to. Only he didn't want to and that told her all she needed to know. She was on the outside with Ruy and always would be.

The limousine dropped them off at an enormous mansion milling with beautifully dressed guests. From the moment she entered she was conscious of female eyes clinging to her. Mercedes made a special point of greeting her again while from every corner Ruy was hailed as though he were a very important guest indeed. Before very long he was the centre of a crush of men, gamely answering every question aimed at him.

'Ruy seems very popular,' she remarked to Mercedes.

'He always has been. That level of success impresses most people. He was also every girl's pin-up when I was at school and he hasn't lost his appeal to the ladies,' Mercedes responded.

'I noticed that he attracted a fair amount of attention at the church,' Suzy admitted uncomfortably.

'It's vulgar, but all the women who made a play for him and got nowhere are madly curious to know what you had that they didn't and why you have that ring on your finger.' Mercedes wrinkled her nose with distaste. 'I'm afraid that Ruy acquired the reputation of being a commitment-phobe.'

'I can't think why.' Suzy laughed although she could taste bitterness behind her fake amusement because Ruy was exactly what everyone had thought he was: a commitment-phobe. She had never been in the running for anything deeper with Ruy. From the outset he had made it clear that he didn't want a relationship and he had stuck to his rules.

Ruy retrieved her and they took their seats and a long elaborate meal began, accompanied by many speeches. It was a relief to get up and stretch her legs on the dance floor afterwards. 'If I ever get married,' Suzy told Ruy, 'there will be no pomp and ceremony to it.'

'Weddings are very much family affairs. The bride and groom don't always have a choice. I have very stuffy relatives. This type of ritual and tradition is exactly what they appreciate and respect. Some of them have come to speak to you today but most of them are too busy observing you and gossiping and they won't officially meet you until tomorrow.'

'You're scaring the life out of me!' Suzy censured, slender hips moving in time to the pulsing beat of the music as she moved back from him.

Another man hovered, requesting permission with a look at Ruy to step in to partner Suzy. Ruy wanted to say no but he was mindful of the occasion and reluctant to act possessive, even knowing that he was hellishly possessive when it came to Suzy. He backed to the edge of the floor, taking the chance to watch her dance, appreciating the fluid grace of every movement, her perfect synchronisation with the music. His replacement moved in with a great deal more panache than Ruy had in the dance department and a wry smile curved his sardonic mouth.

'Who is he?' he asked his brother as he drew level with him.

'Don't you recognise him?' Rigo said in surprise. 'Jorge's a professional…stars in that dance show Mercedes adores on Channel—'

'I don't watch dance shows. Do you think she needs rescuing?' Ruy interrupted, his entire attention glued to Suzy's animated face.

'I don't and maybe you need to let her have some space,' Rigo murmured thoughtfully, turning to study his twin. 'Never thought I'd see you being clingy with a woman.'

'I'm not.'

'Never thought I'd get married again either though,' his twin continued as if Ruy hadn't spoken, a relaxed note to that admission that impressed Ruy. 'But I don't need pills or booze to get through the day with Mercedes around. She lights up my world.'

'Congratulations. I'm very happy for you both.' Ruy breathed in deep and slow, suddenly appreciating how important such an exchange was with his long-lost twin, opening the possibility of a closer, more normal relationship. It heartened him, made him realise how much Suzy's presence had lightened the atmosphere between him and his brother.

At the same time, Rigo's words had made Ruy reluctantly recall his world pre-Suzy. It had been very well organised, and every moment had been scheduled to maximise efficient productivity. He had fallen off that relentless train, however. He didn't think that way any more because Suzy had driven a coach and horses through his schedule. Only now was it dawning on him that in less than twenty-four hours Suzy was leaving and he would be returning to that rigorous cult of maximum efficiency. The prospect was not enticing, not the way he had dimly assumed it would be. She had changed him…somehow she had contrived to change him in a fundamental way…and Ruy was no fan of change or innovation. He was much more likely to fight it off than embrace it.

'Maybe we could meet up for dinner some evening once we get back from our wedding trip,' Rigo said hesitantly. 'Mercedes was very taken with Suzy. '

Ruy was still struggling to deal with the awareness that Suzy would no longer be around the following evening. 'That…that would be good, *great*,' he stressed, endeavouring to express his gratitude for that invite with greater warmth.

Rigo swung away to greet an older man who had grabbed his arm to get his attention. Ruy strode onto the dance floor to reclaim Suzy. She and her partner had gathered an audience with their display and he judged it time to intervene, not because he objected to her dancing or attracting attention, but because he intended to make the most of every moment he had left with her.

'Gosh, that guy was very *intense*,' Suzy hissed, breathing heavily from her dance moves but visibly grateful to leave her partner. 'He wanted me to audition for some television competition show and he was so pushy. I'm not good enough for that sort of thing.'

'I'm no expert but I think you probably are good enough,' Ruy overruled.

'But it's not me. I'm not a performer. I never was. I like teaching kids. I like dance as an exercise but I'm never comfortable with people watching me when I do it,' she whispered. 'It drove my teacher mad when I was a teenager when I wouldn't apply for stuff but that's the way I am.'

'Nothing wrong with that...' Ruy looked askance at her as she pulled away from him.

'I'm hot. I need to freshen up. I won't be long,' she told him, walking off into the crush.

The overpowering plush opulence of the

large cloakroom made her roll her eyes.
Emerging from a stall to wash her hands
at the vanity counter, she jerked in surprise
when she saw an older blonde woman seated
in a chair in the corner and staring at her.
'Sorry, I didn't see you,' she muttered in taut
Spanish.

'I wanted a closer look at the woman Ruy
Valiente is planning to marry,' the blonde informed her, rising from her seat. She was so
thin she was almost emaciated, the bones of
her chest visible through the glittering diamond necklace she wore.

'Why?' Suzy asked baldly as she dried her
hands, rather creeped out by the suspicion
that she was being ambushed on purpose.

'Only a very confident woman could attend this wedding with Ruy and still hold her
head high.'

'And why's that?' Suzy enquired, removing a lipstick from her clutch.

'A decent woman would have been too embarrassed to show her face so boldly. After
all, Ruy slept with Rodrigo's first wife and

she killed herself when he dumped her. It took his brother a very long time to get over that betrayal.'

Suzy was so shocked she was frozen in suspended animation with her lipstick tightly caught between her fingers. The blonde departed with a malicious smile. In a haze of disbelief, Suzy renewed her lipstick and stared into space, blank with shrinking horror at what she had been told. Was it true? It *couldn't* be true! That could not be the reason that Ruy had a troubled relationship with his brother! Ruy could not be guilty of such an indefensible act, she reasoned in consternation.

And yet...*and yet* he had been unwilling to admit the story behind the gossip she had mentioned. Surely only a man ashamed of his past behaviour would behave that way? Rigo's wife had killed herself? After having an affair with Ruy and being ditched? Suzy was appalled at that claim. But she also knew that gossip, even cruel gossip, was often based more on entertainment than fact. She was leaving the cloakroom when Mercedes approached her.

'I saw Elisa Torres coming out looking smug,' she said anxiously. 'Did she speak to you?'

'The skinny blonde with the diamonds?' Suzy checked and nodded. 'She didn't seem friendly.'

'No, she wouldn't be. Elisa's daughter, Fernanda, made a big play for Ruy last year, probably with her mother's encouragement.' Mercedes grimaced. 'There is no man in Spain more likely to be more turned off by a woman chasing him than Ruy and he froze her out. Seeing him engaged to another woman will have enraged Elisa. Did she say anything to you?'

'She said something in Spanish, but she spoke too fast and I didn't catch it. The look on her face was sufficient warning,' Suzy fibbed for the sake of peace, because she knew she could have asked Mercedes for the truth but she had sufficient consideration for the bride's feelings on her special day to swallow her nosy questions. The brunette would not wish to be drawn down that path and it would make her uncomfortable, not only because it was intensely private stuff but also because she had only just met Suzy. In such circumstances, silence was golden.

'That's good, because Elisa is usually critical rather than pleasant,' Mercedes confided, accompanying Suzy back to the main reception room.

For the remainder of their time at the reception, Suzy kept on smiling and trying to behave normally. But the whole time she was stealing stricken glances at Ruy and wondering. Did he? *Could* he have? Could she have fallen in love with a man that immoral, disloyal and seedy?

And the moral of that story was that she had once agreed to marry Percy Brenton, crediting that he was, at heart, a decent enough older man worthy, at least, of her respect and trust. How could she ever have been that gullible about a man who had literally blackmailed her to the altar? Events had proven her to be badly wrong in her naïve assumptions when it came to Percy, she reminded herself painfully.

How much did she really know about Ruy? And did it even matter if he was guilty as charged when their brief affair was virtually over? Why would she confront him now with such explosive accusations? Their relationship as such was already almost over, bar her final departure. Was there any point in stirring up such sordid unpleasantness? Particularly when, with Ruy's stake in her father's pub, she might well be forced to see him again in the future. No, she would keep her lips firmly sealed and endure her curiosity. What else could she do when Ruy had already refused to discuss the gossip she had questioned? Obviously, he didn't want to talk about such sleazy stuff, not now when it was all over. And why would he even want to discuss it with Suzy when he had already made it clear that his past was none of her business?

'You did really well today,' Ruy told her on

the drive back to the *palacio* after midnight. 'Thank you.'

A tense smile curved Suzy's mouth. 'Well, that appearance was what I was here for,' she reminded him quietly.

'You were very convincing,' Ruy continued.

'I must be a better actress than I ever appreciated,' Suzy demurred, relieved that she had less than twenty-four hours left to spend in Spain. Stepping back from Ruy and the level of intimacy they had indulged in was a challenge and to behave normally while accomplishing that feat was an even bigger one.

Her feet were killing her. She wondered if it was a rule that new shoes always had to pinch, but even if she had been warned she would have picked them because they had been the perfect match for her dress. In the marble hall, she kicked them off and lifted them to pad barefoot upstairs.

'I could carry you,' Ruy proposed with amusement.

'Not required.'

She got ready for bed quickly. From below lowered lashes she covertly watched Ruy undress, marvelling at how familiar his every move had become to her. He was so organised, so methodical. Everything had a place, and nothing got lost because it always went back in the same spot. She was the exact opposite but sharing a room with Ruy had made her tidier, not only because that was his preference, but also because she was now mortifyingly aware that in the *palacio*, if she left something on the floor, someone else had to pick it up.

The mattress gave a little with Ruy's weight. The lights went out. He reached for her and she tried not to freeze.

'Er...we *can't*,' she muttered, cheeks burning as she brought out the excuse she needed. 'It's that time of the month.'

The heat of his lean, powerful body spread slowly through the chill that gripped her.

'Not a problem,' Ruy murmured, still holding her close.

Suzy had expected him to let go of her and retreat, but he did neither.

'Are you feeling all right?' he asked, a shade awkwardly.

'I'm not great,' she fibbed.

And he let go of her immediately, switched on the lights, emerged from the dressing room in jeans and left the room. Suzy sat up, wondering where he was going. She lay down again, planning to fake sleep, but a few minutes later Ruy reappeared with tablets and a glass of water, sitting on her side of the bed and feeding them to her. That he would be that considerate hadn't occurred to her and she was embarrassed, forced to swallow pills she didn't need.

'Try to go to sleep,' he urged as he doused the lights again.

He didn't put his arms round her again and, absurdly, she wished he would because it would have been the very last time they were that close. She squeezed her eyes tight shut and ordered her brain to shut down but there was no closing out the revelation that Elisa Torres had made.

Had Ruy fallen in love with his brother's wife? He must've done, she assumed. Surely he would not have betrayed his brother's trust for anything less than an all-encompassing love? And yet it did not excuse him because love didn't turn a sordid affair into a case of Romeo and Juliet. Ultimately, Ruy had ended the relationship but Rigo must still have been devastated. And then his wife had died, and he could hardly have got any sort of closure from that tragic conclusion. She marvelled that Ruy's twin had invited him to his second wedding and could only admire Rigo for his ability to accept the past and forgive.

The next day, she had to work hard at keeping her spirits up. She was determined not to reveal the truth that she was dreading returning home when in reality it was what any sane woman would want after discovering such bad news about the man she cared about. Before lunch, which they would be sharing with Ruy's closest relatives, she laid out the dress she had selected from the rails. It was a dark blue dress that barely showed any skin, extremely conservative. She had picked it after meeting a couple of Ruy's very starchy aunts and uncles at the wedding the previous day. It helped to remember that she was merely fulfilling a pretend role and that in a few hours she would be taking off the truly beautiful ring for ever. None of it was real, she reminded herself doggedly. It was her own foolish fault that she had dived too deep into her first affair even after being warned that it wouldn't be a relationship.

And she had no real grounds for complaint, had she? He had told her with candour that they had no future and he had treated her well and with respect. He hadn't shared his deepest secrets but then who did in a casual fling? If she were discovering that in reality she couldn't do casual comfortably with a man, that was her problem, not his.

Ruy studied her in surprise as she came downstairs. 'You don't look like you in that outfit,' he remarked.

Suzy wrinkled her nose. 'I might as well serve up what your relations like and expect from your future wife. Why ruffle feathers when it's not real?'

'I don't care what they think,' Ruy intoned almost harshly.

'Ruy…you agreed to a fake engagement celebration for their benefit. Of course, you care. You were raised to care, weren't you? You can't help that,' she reasoned.

'I try not to follow my father's rules,' he countered.

'I suppose that family is simply family and your father's rules don't come into it,' Suzy murmured, connecting briefly with his stunning dark golden eyes and feeling her heart pound and her mouth run dry before swiftly evading that direct connection.

He wasn't the man she had believed he was, she reminded herself fiercely, heartbroken at the idea that he could have behaved so badly. He was neither loyal nor trustworthy. He was a cheater, and a man who would cheat with his brother's wife would probably be unfaithful in future relationships as well. Of course, there was a chance that that vindictive woman had been lying, but Ruy's own refusal to discuss the gossip he had acknowledged had convinced Suzy that there had to be a nasty secret in his past, one that, quite understandably, he didn't wish to discuss.

But what sort of judge was she of any man? Particularly after her foolish trust in Percy? That had been a big fail on her part, and she couldn't forget how naïve she had been.

Why was she so angry with Ruy, though? It wasn't as though she had been in the running for something more serious with him. But she was disappointed in him, disappointed in herself, convinced that she should have sensed that moral vacuum inside him or at least suspected that Ruy didn't share her basic moral values. That discovery made him a lot less desirable, she told herself firmly. Or at least it should've done, she registered, gripped with anguish when he closed his hand over hers to walk her out onto the formal loggia where drinks and coffee awaited them following the leisurely lunch, which under Manuel's watch was conducted with many courses and great ceremony.

Time was running out for her and Ruy like sand running through an egg timer, leading to the inevitable separation. But if she had any real pride, she would be eager to leave him, she told herself urgently. It didn't help that she was simply devastated to credit that he could have slept with his brother's wife.

'I wish Cecile hadn't had to work. She always lightens the atmosphere on her visits,' Ruy breathed with a frown, but his tolerance also showed her that he was very generous towards his demanding relatives. 'You seem very…stressed, tense—'

'I haven't much experience of being on show like this,' Suzy pointed out in a taut whisper, drawing her head back from his proximity as the achingly familiar scent of his cologne and his skin enveloped her. 'And why *would* Cecile have made the effort to attend? She knows that this event is only an unlucky consequence of you having persuaded me to act a part at your brother's wedding. She knows we're a fake.'

'Not quite as fake as you're suggesting when I don't want you to go home,' Ruy disconcerted her by declaring with the utmost calm. 'I want you to stay.'

Utterly taken aback by that astonishing statement, Suzy momentarily froze. 'You're not done painting me yet?' she hazarded with a stilted laugh.

'Probably not but that's not the only reason,' Ruy breathed, shooting her a narrow-eyed appraisal that questioned her attitude. 'What's the matter with you?'

'I suppose I'm homesick. I can't wait to see Dad,' Suzy exclaimed in desperation, ranging away a few feet from his tall, still frame, determined not to let him pierce her defences, weak as they were.

'You won't consider remaining here with me?' Ruy prompted on a dangerous note, his dark deep accented drawl dropping in pitch, purring down her spine like a caress.

Suzy lifted her chin. 'It's not possible. I think we've run our course, don't you?'

And with that she lifted the coffee poured for her and strolled away. It wasn't hard to sidestep Ruy in a family gathering. As soon as she stepped away, his relations closed in and clumped around him like a wall, full of deference and desperate for his attention. They told him about business upsets, family problems and financial challenges. Over lunch he had promised to check out the fiancé one of the daughters was planning to marry, had agreed to look over a cousin's business plan and had promised to contact a friend to help a son find a suitable job. It was ironic that she had begun to see exactly how Ruy had developed his arrogant belief that he could solve every problem in her path. His family had convinced him that he was all-seeing, all-knowing, the ultimate oracle.

Even so, his tolerance of those same demands impressed her with his generosity although she did see why he guarded his privacy because his relatives recognised few boundaries.

Yet how had those same prim and prudish aunts and uncles overlooked his behaviour with Rodrigo's first wife? Had they simply closed their eyes? Did their reverence for his social position, his wealth and his spectacular success excuse every flaw he had in their estimation?

The younger generation of his many cousins chatted casually to her and she talked freely to them, admitting that she hadn't had the chance to further her education but that she was still hoping to rectify that oversight. But at the back of her mind, she couldn't really think of anything but Ruy and the suggestion he had made that she stay on in Spain in his home.

What on earth was he proposing? And why had he waited until the eleventh hour to mention it? Of course, the wedding had taken up the whole of the previous day and evening and there had not been an opportunity for them to talk about anything serious. But then,

Ruy didn't *do* serious, so what was he talking about? She had a life to live and it wasn't in Spain. Most probably he found their liaison convenient. The sex was off-the-charts amazing and wasn't that, according to popular report, what the average guy reputedly valued the most? In addition, she made no demands on him. High colour mantled her cheeks at the humiliation of such thoughts in which she was reduced to rating her precise value like some product and she lifted her bright head high as she smiled at the last departing guests.

'Now perhaps you'll tell me what's wrong with you,' Ruy breathed in the marble hall.

'I have to pack,' Suzy told him with urgency.

Impervious to the hint that she intended to be very busy, Ruy followed her upstairs. He strode into the bedroom. 'I ask you to stay on and you don't even want to discuss it?' he pressed incredulously.

'It's not possible,' Suzy told him, hauling her case out in the dressing room, wishing he weren't able to see that it was almost fully packed already. 'Thank you for the offer but I'm saying no, we're done.'

'Why?' Ruy demanded rawly, swiping the heavy case from her and planting it noisily down on the luggage rack in the bedroom. 'Why wouldn't it be possible?'

Suzy felt trapped. She hadn't wanted such a confrontation, had seen no advantage to it, indeed had only foreseen future repercussions. 'It just wouldn't be,' she muttered evasively.

She yanked comfy clothes out of her case and carried them into the bathroom, closing and locking the door for privacy.

'I want... I *need* an answer,' Ruy growled outside the door.

Suzy stripped off the dress and pulled on yoga pants and a loose sleeveless sweatshirt. She was all shaky. She didn't want to leave the bathroom, but she was no coward. Breathing in deep, she padded out again barefoot, to head back to her case to dig out canvas shoes.

'I don't want to talk about this with you,' she warned him stiffly.

'I'm afraid you have no choice but to talk about it. That jet won't take off until I get an answer,' Ruy spelt out flatly.

That hard assurance warned her that there was no way she would be getting home without satisfying his curiosity, but she was still very reluctant to tackle so controversial a topic with a male she knew to be fiercely private and determined not to confide in her.

'Suzy...' Ruy breathed.

As she looked at him involuntarily, it was as if a cruel hand squeezed her heart inside her tight chest. Black hair slightly tousled, a dark shadow of stubble accentuating his jaw and sensual mouth, his dark eyes smouldering gold, he was rawly masculine and very much the man she had fallen madly in love with. She had become accustomed to the man in the sharply tailored business suits that he wore with such panache. At first that sophisticated image had intimidated her, and then he had simply become *her* Ruy and what he wore and where he lived and how much money he had hadn't mattered to her any longer. When he had rescued her and her father from Percy, when he had supported her through that frightening experience, she had begun to believe that Ruy Valiente was everything she had ever wanted in a man. Discovering that he was not that man had shattered her faith in her own judgement.

She straightened her shoulders, lifted her head, green eyes veiled. 'Is it true that you slept with your brother's first wife and that she…er…died when you ditched her?'

As she'd spoken, Ruy had become as still as a statue, his lean dark features wiped clean of all expression, but his healthy colour had evaporated and his shock stabbed her to the heart because she took that reaction as confirmation. He compressed his lips and it took a few seconds for him to master his surprise at that question and respond. 'In essence the facts can be interpreted in that light. People who know me are aware of the true facts and if you knew me better—'

'I don't *want* to know you any better!' Suzy let loose at him because her tension had climbed and climbed unbearably while she awaited his answer and the ferocious disillusionment she suffered at his lack of argument did not make her feel generous. 'What I was told convinced me that I want nothing more to do with you!'

Suzy was devastated when he failed to contradict her. She had hoped against hope that he would have an explanation, a miraculous excuse, but then that weak hope only reminded her of how poor her own judgement was and of how she could not trust her own feelings. She might love him but that did not automatically mean that he was a decent person. Hadn't she once believed that Percy was decent too? That unfortunate acknowledgement tore her down even further in her estimation.

'That is, of course, your choice even if I'm surprised that you would be so judgemental when you can be in possession of few facts,' Ruy retorted icily.

A kind of rage more powerful than anything Ruy had ever felt before was roaring through him. Liliana had forced him to live through a nightmare and she had cost him and his unfortunate brother so much. He refused to believe that her spectre could cost him Suzy as well. 'You believed whatever seedy gossip you were told, then.'

'I didn't want to, but, yes, I believed it because you wouldn't discuss anything private with me, which implied that there *was* something shameful in your past.'

'Everyone's got something shameful in their past, Suzy,' Ruy incised with gritty cynicism at such innocence, and his rage was now roaring inside him like a forest blaze. 'But logic should tell you that things aren't always what they seem.'

'I don't want to hear some devious explanation that paints *you* white and *her* scarlet! That such a thing ever happened is unpardonable. It should be enough for me to say that I can't be with a guy capable of behaving that way,' Suzy framed in a pained rush.

Ruy was outraged, deeply offended and hurt by her complete lack of trust in him. His deep anger and his ferocious pride drove him, preventing him from making any further attempt to explain himself or reason with her. 'Then I too have nothing more to say,' he bit out with savage brevity.

The silence stretched thick as a blanket and it felt claustrophobic. Pain burning inside her, Suzy gazed silently back at him, willing him to pull a miracle out of his pocket and fix everything but somehow knowing now that that wasn't going to happen. She felt sick and she simply nodded on the least said, soonest mended rule because his past was still not really her business. And any prospect of it being her business had died when that horrible woman had made her sordid allegations and Ruy had then confirmed the facts.

'I'll finish packing, then,' she said jerkily.

He walked out of the door. If he had slammed it, she would have felt a little better, but he didn't. She removed the diamond ring on her finger and set it on the dresser. She left the green dress and the blue one she had worn that afternoon over a chair because she wanted no reminders. Didn't need them, she conceded wretchedly. She suspected that it would be a very long time before she forgot Ruy Valiente and the happiness he had given her before she'd discovered that it was all as much of an illusion as their fake engagement.

CHAPTER TEN

'YOU CAN SIT in the car while I nip into the off-licence,' her father wheedled. 'Save me parking across the road.'

'You usually go on your own… I'm kind of busy here,' Suzy argued, barely lifting her head from the academic website she was studying.

Roger Madderton frowned down at his daughter. 'I'll be blunt, then. *I'm* tired of you moping about the place like a wet weekend. Two weeks of that is enough. You need to get out of the flat, even come down and help behind the bar—'

'Flora's managing fine,' Suzy reminded her parent stiffly, because it had been something of a shock to discover on her return that her place had been filled more than adequately by the older woman, who was also cooking up a storm of popular meals to sell to their weekend customers. That had stung when Suzy had only contrived to serve up pizzas and paninis, her catering skills being rather more basic.

And then there had been the mortification of all the tales about Percy Brenton that had come her way whenever she was seen. The locals seemed to think it was their bounden duty to tell her anything that related to her ex. Percy had been charged and arrested. As soon as he had got out on bail, he had put his house on the market and he had not been seen since. There was a rumour that his assault on Suzy had not been his first offence and that he had a bitter ex-wife now living in York. It didn't seem to occur to anyone that Suzy couldn't have cared less and that she was merely grateful not to have to see the man again.

'Come on,' her father urged, and with great reluctance Suzy rose from her seat at the desk in the lounge of the flat and followed him downstairs to his car.

She *wasn't* moping, she thought resentfully. She had done her best to be cheerful and helpful since she came home. But most of her attention had been reserved for the different educational courses available to anyone planning to work with children. The variety of options had made it hard to choose because she wasn't sure how high to set her sights or whether or not to settle on a short course or a lengthier one. In short, she had done everything possible to avoid moping and stay busy and if she was miserable she had done her best to hide the fact.

A broken heart was a broken heart, and she couldn't eat or sleep without thinking about Ruy and feeling a great gush of pain and hollowness engulf her until she felt as if she were drowning.

In truth she had left her heart behind in Spain and she remained furious in her bitterness with Ruy. He hadn't wanted her enough to fight for her! He hadn't wanted her enough to defend himself! It was even more galling that she had shut him down before he was forced to define exactly what he had meant by asking her to stay in Spain with him. After all, if you didn't have a relationship to begin with how did one move on from that point, particularly with the complication of a fake engagement in play? Yes, Suzy would very much have enjoyed hearing Ruy explain what he was asking her to consider. Not, of course, that she *could* have overlooked what she had discovered about him, but she was only human, she would still have liked to *know.*

Her father was unusually quiet on his way to the off-licence and when he emerged she was surprised that he was only carrying a little crate of beer.

'That was a small order,' she remarked as he reversed the car and drove off again.

On the drive home, she said, 'Have I really been that hard to live with?'

Roger Madderton groaned. 'You're inconsolable. How am I expected to feel as your dad? I want to fix it for you.'

'You can't fix it. He wasn't the guy I thought

he was,' Suzy sighed, patting his knee sooth-ingly. 'I'll get over this. Don't worry about me.'

'I can help you fix it,' her father asserted, disconcerting her. 'You're very stubborn. He's very stubborn as well but he's also a few years older and a little less short-sighted than you can be.'

'Why are you talking about Ruy like this?' Suzy twisted in her seat as her father turned off the road down a familiar lane. 'Why are we driving down here?'

Her father stopped at the electric gates that secured Ruy's house in the woods. The gates whirred open and Suzy stared in disbelief at her parent while he marvelled out loud at the camera-recognition technology that had given them automatic entry.

'Dad!' she gasped in frustration. 'What are we doing here?'

'You had a row with him, and you didn't talk it out. This is your last chance to get it sorted,' her father told her squarely.

At the realisation that Ruy was back in England, Suzy froze in consternation. 'I'm not going in there!'

'If he's made the effort to fly over here, you can make the effort to at least listen to what he has to say. You don't have to forgive him for whatever he's done,' her father pointed out levelly.

'I can't believe you're doing this to me!' Suzy protested, shooting him a shaken glance.

'I hope you don't still feel that way in ten minutes—'

'Ten minutes?'

'I'll wait here for ten minutes. If you aren't back out again by then I'll go home.' Her father switched off the engine with a flourish.

'Did Ruy somehow force you into doing this for him?'

'No, he was planning to come to the pub, but I didn't want to find myself in the middle of your drama and it's not very private there. This is the better option,' Roger Madderton opined and leant across her to swing open the passenger door in invitation.

Suzy snatched in a sustaining breath and leapt out. 'I'll be out in less than ten minutes!'

'Famous last words, my love,' her father said equably as she slammed the door shut again.

Furious with Ruy for using her dad to do his bidding and mysteriously contriving to shift the older man's loyalty away from his daughter, Suzy stomped up the steps. Ruy opened the door himself and her heart skipped a beat straight away. His black hair was still damp from the shower, his jawline freshly shaven. Sheathed in jeans and a shirt, he should have seemed familiar but he was definitely changed with his lean, strong face rather fined down, his spectacular dark eyes under-shadowed. Her first thought was that he had been ill, and alarm clutched at her and only with the greatest difficulty did she resist the urge to demand proof of his health.

'Ruy...' It was all she could do to squeeze those syllables from her dry throat.

'Don't blame your father for this. I phoned

him last night and persuaded him that this meeting was for the best.'

'But it's not,' Suzy whispered, sidling past him, careful not to brush against him.

'Hear me out and *then* say that,' Ruy framed harshly.

What Suzy wasn't about to say to him was that seeing him again and refreshing her memories only made their separation more painful for her. 'OK,' she agreed. 'I'll listen.'

Ruy strode into the spacious reception area. 'I told you about my stalking ordeal eight years ago.'

'Well, you didn't tell me how you settled it,' Suzy remarked in a brittle voice.

'I didn't settle it, but eventually I involved the police and she was charged. I had to do something. The longer it went on, the worse it became. She assaulted a woman I took out to dinner. When the police arrested her and searched her apartment they discovered that she had gathered a huge amount of information about me long before I met her. She had deliberately targeted me in the club the night we met.'

Suzy was frowning. 'That's creepy. What happened to the poor woman she assaulted?'

'She was shaken up, but she managed to get away from her. Although I was convinced it was my stalker who had attacked her, we weren't able to prove it. The assault made me bring in the police,' Ruy admitted. 'After she was arrested, her parents approached me and begged me to drop the charges. They said the prosecution would ruin her life. They promised to get her psychiatric treatment and swore that I would never see her again. I dropped the charges and to this day, I don't know whether that was the right or wrong thing to do.'

'I don't understand what all this has to do with your brother's wife—'

'Bear with me,' Ruy cut in. 'Would you like a drink?'

'A white wine.'

Ruy filled a glass for her, his lean brown hands deft, and she watched him, studying his sculpted profile, his black hair gleaming as it dried in the sunlight arrowing through the tall windows. 'I was sympathetic towards my stalker's parents because my brother also had mental-health issues,' Ruy explained. 'Rigo had a nervous breakdown in his teens. He got hooked on prescription drugs and eventually he had to go into rehab to get clean. Six months after that he phoned me to tell me that he had got engaged and that he wanted me to meet his future wife, whom he had met in the same clinic. He was besotted with her. She *was* a beautiful woman. Her name was Liliana, my former stalker.'

'Good grief!' Suzy croaked, finally grasping the connection. 'What did you do when you realised?'

'I was honest with him. I told him that I had had a one-night stand with her, which quite naturally angered and upset him. No man wants the woman he loves to have already slept with his brother. I also gave Rigo chapter and verse on her stalking activities and I went to see her parents and asked them to be honest with him as well. They flat out refused. They believed Liliana was in love with my brother and that he was the best chance she had of a normal life. At the same time Liliana gave Rigo some nonsensical story about how I had led her down the garden path and broken her heart, which of course made him sympathetic towards her. I, on the other hand, was convinced she had chosen him *because* he was my brother...and in the end I was proven right on that score.'

Suzy gulped down a mouthful of wine. 'She really did put you through the mill. What happened?'

'He married her, and she began to stalk me again. She was very manipulative. My brother accused me of trying to lure her away from him when I would have done anything to be rid of her attentions!' Ruy admitted in a driven undertone. 'But, no, I certainly never wished her dead. She interrupted a business lunch I was having one day...my brother's wife, my sister-in-law, walking in and draping herself over me as though we were lovers. Her behaviour caused a great deal of talk and I warned Rigo that he had to rein her in or that I would take steps to keep her away from me.'

'My word, Ruy…she made your life hell.' Suzy sighed, understanding all at once why Ruy was so set on not getting into relationships. Liliana had scared him off and had probably made him wary and distrustful of every woman he met after her. 'And your brother's too.'

'The last time I saw her I tried very hard to persuade her to see a psychiatrist and I told her that there was no chance of her ever having a relationship with me, but she became hysterical and I had to drop the subject. That afternoon she bribed a cleaner to gain access to my apartment and took an overdose there,' Ruy related grimly. 'She knew my schedule and usually I would have been home that evening but a crisis had arisen and I flew to Brussels instead.'

Guessing the ending of his story, Suzy

winced. 'Oh, Ruy,' she muttered, pained on his behalf and his brother's.

Dark eyes grim, he compressed his lips. 'I don't believe that she meant to kill herself. I think it was another cry for attention and a desire to punish me. She expected me to find her and get her to a doctor in time. Unfortunately, she wasn't discovered until the next day by which time it was too late. Rigo blamed me for her death.'

'I don't see how he could,' Suzy breathed, troubled at that unjust bestowal of blame in such tragic circumstances.

'He had to blame someone...why not me? As he saw it, I had stolen his wife's affections, treated her with cruel indifference and destroyed her mental health. I tried to reason with him, but he was too bitter back then.'

'It wasn't your fault.'

'Wasn't it? Perhaps had I been a little more discerning the night I met her, I would have spent more time talking to her and then I might have realised that we were not suited in any way.'

'I don't think that would have mattered when she had already fixated on you. I'm sorry I misjudged you,' Suzy said truthfully. 'I shouldn't have listened to gossip.'

'None of us should but we all do it,' Ruy murmured wryly.

'I didn't trust my own faith in you because of what Percy did to me,' Suzy admitted in a shamed rush. 'You see, I trusted him once too and then I realised how foolish I had been and, after that, I didn't see how I could trust you...particularly when you seemed too good to be true.'

'I like the sound of being too good to be true,' Ruy confided.

Suzy went pink. 'We were talking about Liliana and your brother,' she reminded him. 'I think she married Rigo simply to get closer to you. She used him.'

'Although it's taken him years of therapy to get over her, he's stronger now and Mercedes is, thankfully, a very different woman. Now I want to show you something...' Ruy paused at the foot of the stairs and regarded her expectantly, a catch in his usually level dark drawl, almost a slight hint of nervousness. 'Your portrait.'

'You finished it?' Suzy prompted eagerly, springing up to approach him.

'It's upstairs.'

He cast open the bedroom door and there it was, resting on an easel by the window in the far corner. Suzy slowly crossed the room to stand in front of the vivid image and study it with wondering eyes. Her hair and her skin seemed luminescent. She looked as though she were about to leap off the bench and walk right out of the painting. It was an extraordinary likeness. 'You've made me look as though I'm beautiful, though,' she whispered self-consciously. 'And I'm not.'

Ruy smiled. '*Sí, querida*...you are. And you destroyed my artistic objectivity. You modelled for my very first romantic portrait.'

'You don't do romantic,' she reminded him.

'I do for you. I do a lot of things differently with you,' Ruy murmured, reaching for her left hand and showing her the diamond ring he was holding as he dropped down very deliberately on one knee. 'Will you do me the very great honour of becoming my wife?'

Thoroughly taken aback by that proposal of marriage, Suzy stared down into anxious dark golden eyes and she dropped down onto her knees as well, covering his lean, strong face with kisses and grabbing the ring in the midst of it. In fact it was a bit of a free-for-all between him trying to get the ring back on her finger at the same time as he claimed her mouth in a fierce ravaging kiss designed to prove to her that she was being claimed for all time as his.

'Oh, my goodness, Ruy… I love you so much and I wasn't expecting that…but we've only known each other a few weeks,' she exclaimed in reluctant protest.

'If I had known what love felt like I'd have proposed the first day but I hadn't ever been in love before so I didn't recognise what I was feeling,' Ruy explained, appraising her dazed face with adoring intensity. 'At first I assumed it was an overwhelming desire to paint you. But I needed to keep you close as well and prevent anyone and anything from ever hurting you. I wanted to kill Brenton… slowly. I wanted to wake up with you in the morning and go to sleep with you beside me every night. I didn't just fall in love with you a little. I fell obsessively in love with you.'

'That's good…that's good. Stop saying it as if it's peculiar when it's not. I thought I would break in two leaving you behind in Spain because it hurt so much.' Suzy framed his lean dark face with unsteady hands. 'And you didn't try to *stop* me leaving!'

'I was so angry that you could believe me capable of such sleazy behaviour, angry… and, *sí*—' he sighed '—also hurt. I expected you to have more faith in me.'

Suzy flinched at that quiet admission. 'I didn't trust my own judgement enough after Percy,' she confided heavily as she closed both arms round him with so much determination that she almost toppled him. 'But I swear I'm getting over that now…and look at you, I can see that you haven't been sleeping, you haven't been looking after yourself properly...*and* you've lost weight!' she condemned with ringing disapproval.

'Our chef is grieving your absence. I've eaten Thai, Malaysian, Vietnamese, Indonesian, Indian and Mexican dishes every day you've been gone and not one British or Spanish meal. I need you at home with me so that I can eat again and regulate the menu. I need you round the clock.'

'But marriage—'

'And soon,' Ruy urged as he lifted her up off the floor and brought her down on the welcome softness of the bed. 'Like really, *really* soon, like possibly this week, and a casual, relaxed wedding that you would like here with your father and Cecile and her family attending. And then possibly a more traditional do for Spain and the rest of my family. You get to pick your own wedding dress too and it doesn't have to have feathers.'

'You *are* insane,' Suzy told him lovingly as he came down over her. She speared her fingers happily into his tousled black hair. 'I'm going to drive you nuts sometimes…you do know that? I'm untidy and impulsive and—'

'You are the woman I love, and I can't do without you in my life another day,' Ruy swore vehemently.

'I've got so used to you too. I thought I disliked so much about you, but you made me feel safe, protected, *cared* for even though I fought with you about your bossiness,' Suzy told him, hauling him down to kiss her again, revelling in the weight of his body on hers. 'I couldn't believe how much I missed you. I fell like a ton of bricks for you and now you're going to be stuck with me and my irritating habits for ever.'

'You wouldn't believe how good for ever sounds,' Ruy admitted with a brilliant smile.

'But you didn't do serious relationships! How has this happened?'

'Liliana scared me off. I saw how devastated Rigo was by her betrayal. And her death. I thought it was safer to keep my distance from deeper relationships with women and that then I could control things. But you broke through my defences, you made me want stuff I had never wanted before…and I wanted you more than anything I had ever wanted in my life and all of a sudden nothing else mattered. Not my pride and not all the anger and bitterness I had suppressed over Liliana. I suppose, a little like my brother, I was ready to make a fresh start and there you were in your tatty wedding dress, swinging those ridiculous boots over the edge of that tree-house platform and being very cheeky.'

Suzy grinned and traced a fingertip along his full lower lip. 'And you *like* cheeky.'

'I didn't know that until you fell into my arms in the woods.'

'That's not how it happened!' Suzy argued, her pride stung by that claim.

'Technically it is and you smelled so good and felt so amazing in my arms, *mi corazón,*' Ruy husked, running the very tip of his tongue along the finger she still had resting against his lips. 'I started to fall for you that same moment, but when you did that handstand in the middle of a modelling session I knew I was definitely in trouble.'

'How?'

Ruy dealt her a look of wicked amusement. 'I would have strangled any other model who pulled a stunt like that but when you did it, I thought it was cute,' he confessed with a chuckle. '*Cute!* Should've realised that I was in love with you then.'

'You're my first love too,' Suzy admitted, her hands sliding below his shirt to find the silky skin of his long smooth back, making him flex against her and grind his hips into hers.

That was the sole invitation that Ruy required to ravish her parted lips with his and before very long the breathless kisses they exchanged were interspersed by impatient attempts to rid themselves of their clothes without separating their bodies. And when that was finally accomplished, and they lay skin to skin, there was no more conversation. They made love with frantic passionate energy and lay in each other's arms afterwards, sated and blessed with a quiet sense of having finally come home.

'So you want to get married this week,' Suzy remarked when she had her breath back enough to talk. 'You realise that there are formalities that have to be met?'

'Special licence…already have it in the pipeline.' Ruy dealt her a victorious look. 'I never suggest anything I can't do.'

'I'll wear the feather dress… I loved it and you painting me in it made it kind of special,' Suzy told him dreamily. 'And I may just be persuaded to borrow the small diamond tiara in that family jewel chest you let me rake through—it was very pretty.'

'Do you want children?'

'Oh, at least a dozen!' she replied.

'A dozen?' Ruy exclaimed in disbelief.

'Well, more than one, less than ten. I always kind of saw myself with a little team of kids. You should have asked that question *before* you proposed,' Suzy pointed out with a grin. 'You look so horrified. We can negotiate. Don't worry about it.'

As a slender hand ran down appreciatively over his abdomen, Ruy discovered that he didn't have it in him to worry about anything at all. *'Te amo, tesora mia.'*

Suzy sat up in sudden dismay. 'Oh, my goodness, I left Dad sitting outside in his car and forgot about him!'

Ruy tugged her lazily down to him again. 'He had driven off before I even brought you up here. I told him I was proposing.'

'Oh...' Suzy flopped back. 'It's going to be a constant game of one-upmanship with you, isn't it?'

Ruy kissed her again and she forgot to talk.

EPILOGUE

Four years later

'I'M AMAZED RUY let that painting out of the *palacio* from its place of honour at the top of the stairs,' Mercedes teased as she glanced at the huge portrait of Suzy at the centre of the exhibition, the one of her in her feather dress in the orange grove. 'Rigo had to really work on him to get him to loan it out for this and he's gnashing his teeth now because he could have sold it ten times over! And, of course, Ruy will not sell a picture of you to anyone.'

'Or of Mateo,' Suzy added, thinking warmly of her two-year-old son and of the pair of little girls she was currently carrying.

It was only a few weeks since the gender scan and only a couple of weeks more since she had learned that she had conceived twins.

Her pregnancy with Mateo had been easy but the twin one was proving a little tougher in terms of nausea and tiredness and she would be glad when her due date arrived. Although she was wildly excited at the prospect of two little girls to dress, she adored her son. He was a black-haired dark-eyed little replica of his father, full of energy and personality. She was already wondering what the girls she was carrying would be like and was considering the names Rosa, after her own mother, and Ramona, after Ruy's late mother. She liked names with a family connection.

'We wouldn't ever sell the one Ruy did of Javier either.' Mercedes laughed, mentioning her little boy, who was barely six months older than Mateo. 'I don't know how he got either of the boys to sit still long enough for him—'

'He made me amuse them. I tried balloons and that was a disaster, so were the bubbles because the boys got up to chase them, but turning handstands worked and plain bribery worked. Your son is particularly fond of ice cream with multicoloured sprinkles. Mateo's more into crisps.'

'It meant so much to Rodrigo that Ruy came out as V at his gallery with that first exhibition he allowed him to put on for him. That's when the frost really started to melt between them,' the curvy brunette opined.

'Or it could have been the fact that we simply ignored the frost and kept on forcing them together by making dinner dates!' Suzy commented with dancing eyes, loving above all things that, along with Ruy, she had married into a happy family. Rigo had also finally met Cecile and a cautious friendship was beginning to grow between him and the half-sister whom he had once refused to acknowledge.

Mercedes had become Suzy's best friend, always ready to offer advice in the early days of Suzy's marriage when she had been less sure of herself dealing with Ruy's relatives and entertaining. That they were almost the same age, married to brothers and both had young children had undoubtedly helped as well. Suzy's Spanish had come on by leaps and bounds once she was living in Spain.

Ruy had retained the house in Norfolk but he had had to extend it to accommodate their family. Their last wedding anniversary had been spent in England and Suzy had been stunned when Ruy took her through the woods to show her the tree house he had had built. It was a monster of a construction with proper stairs and loads of safety features and Mateo was going to love it when he was old enough to use it. It had provided Suzy with yet another glimpse of her husband's essentially romantic and passionate soul. He had been determined to commemorate that meeting of theirs in the woods when she had been so rude to him.

When they were in England, Suzy spent time with her father and Cecile's family. Roger Madderton was now in a relationship with Flora's daughter, Maddie, a divorcee, who had recently moved to the village. Suzy liked the effervescent blonde and reckoned that it was past time her father found someone of his own.

After the court case in which Percy had been fined for assault, Suzy had heard no more of the older man. He had sold up his businesses locally and moved. Ruy had bought up those same businesses and they were thriving since the opening of the stately home to tourists. He had also financed the rebuilding of the community hall after the place was vandalised and set on fire.

'What's wrong?' Mercedes whispered and then followed the direction of Suzy's eyes.

'*Dios mio*…leaving Ruy alone is like setting down a roast chicken in front of sharks!' the brunette exclaimed.

At least four very beautiful women were circling Suzy's husband and striking poses.

'Every one of them wants to become his next model because featuring in a V painting gives you a definite cachet.'

'And here I am, obviously pregnant and not at my sleekest and they think this is a good time to pounce and try and tempt him,' Suzy completed darkly. 'Excuse me...'

Ruy was talking to an art critic, quite impervious to the predators hovering nearby. Suzy slid a possessive arm through his and he smiled down at her before continuing his conversation. Moments later he pulled away from the other man and leant down to Suzy to say, 'Are you feeling all right? You're a little flushed.'

'I'm pulling the possessive-wife intervention because other women are hovering hoping to steal your attention.'

'You are the only woman who gets my attention, today and every day,' Ruy countered with amusement. 'And well you know it, *mi vida*.'

Suzy stared up at him with a glow of appreciation in her eyes, thinking of how much he had changed from the man she had first met. For a start, he was infinitely more relaxed and less driven. A wife and a child had given Ruy another focus and had taught him that neither art nor finance were the be-all and end-all of life. As for Suzy, she had never known that she could be so happy or so contented.

Later that evening, she studied Mateo as he slept at an angle across his junior bed, the covers heaped on the floor. He was a very restless sleeper. He looked angelic with his ruffled hair and fan-shaped lashes resting on his flushed cheeks, something he never looked awake because he was full of mischief.

Ruy paused in the doorway of the nursery and then crossed the room to scoop her off her feet. 'You're tired,' he told her. 'You were standing too long.'

'If you've got legs, you can't escape standing,' Suzy scoffed as he settled her down on the sofa at the foot of their bed. 'I'm not an invalid.'

Ruy knelt at her feet, sliding a very high shoe off one slender foot and gently flexing her crushed toes. 'I don't know why you bother with shoes like these.'

Suzy knew but she didn't tell him. He loved her legs, he particularly loved them when shod in glitzy heels. As the other foot received the same gentle treatment, she wriggled the zip down on her dress with its cowl neckline. A silk and lace apricot and grey bra came into view, a bra she filled to capacity when she was pregnant. The dress slid to her waist. Eyes burnished with heat, Ruy vaulted upright. Suzy stood, shimmied her hips so that the dress fell away and revealed matching panties. He breathed in deep.

'You are so beautiful, *mi corazón*,' her husband husked with pride and satisfaction.

He believed it too, she thought fondly, and even she had come to believe that, in his eyes, she *was* beautiful. He lifted her up in his arms and crushed her mouth hungrily under his, his tongue stabbing deep, sending a flare of white-hot excitement shafting through her. There was no more talk now of her tiredness. Sometimes Ruy's protectiveness got in the way of her need to be a desirable woman but triggering his hot-blooded nature always overcame that obstacle.

'*Dios, me encantas*...you enchant me, *mi preciosa*,' he husked. 'I love you.'

'To the moon and back,' she slotted in. 'For ever and ever.'

Ruy brought her down gently on the bed and dealt her an appreciative smile. 'You always have to get in that final word...'

But Suzy had always known that she could safely leave that final word to him.

* * * * *

LET'S TALK

Romance

For exclusive extracts, competitions
and special offers, find us online:

f facebook.com/millsandboon

⊙ @millsandboonuk

🐦 @millsandboon

Or get in touch on 0844 844 1351*

For all the latest titles coming soon,
visit millsandboon.co.uk/nextmonth

Want even more
ROMANCE?

Join our bookclub today!

'Mills & Boon books, the perfect way to escape for an hour or so.'

Miss W. Dyer

'Excellent service, promptly delivered and very good subscription choices.'

Miss A. Pearson

'You get fantastic special offers and the chance to get books before they hit the shops'

Mrs V. Hall

Visit millsandbook.co.uk/Bookclub and save on brand new books.

MILLS & BOON